The Elijah Project 2
A New Season

The Elijah Project 2, A New Season

Copyright © 2018, 2019 by Andrea M. Polnaszek, LCSW

All rights reserved. No part of this publication may be reproduced, stored in a retrieval system, or transmitted in any form or by any means – electronic, mechanical, photocopy, recording, or any other – except for brief quotations in printed reviews, without the prior permission of the author.

Artwork created by Matthew Reddy

Graphic designer: Lisa Hardy

Assistant to the author: Renee Wurzer

Printed in the United States of America

ISBN 978-1-7329824-3-7

Dedication

It is with deep gratitude that I dedicate this book to my parents: Miriam and William Boylan. When my parents decided to do life together in 1964 they stood on the firm foundation of their faith. My mother had grown up in a pastor's home and breathed faith from the time she was young. My father had a radical conversion while serving in the United States Army. Together they shepherded the Byfield Parish Church for nearly 50 years. I am forever grateful for their life of faithful service to others and their commitment to Christ through the seasons of their lives.

Table of Contents

Introduction 1

Spring: Dream
Chapter 1: We're Making a Movie 13
Chapter 2: Tyrian Purple 17
Chapter 3: Budding 19

Summer: Development
Chapter 4: We Made a Movie 25
Chapter 5: Growing Up Royal 29
Chapter 6: Growing 33

Fall: Disappointment
Chapter 7: Back to School 39
Chapter 8: When the Castle Can't Protect You 43
Chapter 9: Scarring 47

Winter: Death
Chapter 10: Dark and Cold 53
Chapter 11: When the Castle is All You Know 55
Chapter 12: Brittle 59

Sacred Seasons
Chapter 13: The Season You Find Yourself In 69
Chapter 14: Seasons of Emotion 75
Chapter 15: Seasons of the Spirit 81
Chapter 16: Seasons of Grief 87
Chapter 17: Seasons of Life 97
Chapter 18: Seasons and Your Tree 107
Chapter 19: Seasons of Reflection 115
Chapter 20: The Power of Your Season 127

Resources 135

Scripture References 137

About the Author 141

Preface

Two significant experiences pressed me to write this book. The first sign came while driving to Portland, Oregon on a family vacation. The car was silent; my husband and children slept as I drove from North Dakota into Montana, the landscape transforming from plains to mountains. The ranges spanned as far as the eye could see. As I drove, I imagined. I processed the story of Elijah and envisioned him hiding in the butte like mountain ranges. My mind tucked him into the cavernous terrain away from harm. It was during this drive that I received a word on what was to come. I felt God say:

> "I have three books for you to write: The first you have written, the original, *The Elijah Project: My Protector, My Provider*. The second book will be about Jezebel's back story, how Jezebel becomes Jezebel and ends up going down in history as one of the most evil women ever. This book will provide you an opportunity to incorporate your education on trauma, family patterns, and behavioral choice. The third book will be about legacy, capturing Elijah's story as it intersects with Elisha, extending his earthly ministry two fold. It will explore his journey toward his ultimate whirlwind trip into heaven. This book will be about how to live in the heaven and earth paradox."

I began to imagine the stories and the books. My number one mode of processing is to journal. I write down all my experiences, emotions, and feelings—which of course is difficult if not impossible to do while driving. So for hours I mulled over the vision God had given me. Once my driving shift was over I scribbled the ideas down, writing as clearly as I could in a moving vehicle. I was inspired and excited; I was ready to start writing. Following our vacation real life resumed with heavy job expectations and those journal entries became a faint memory.

A few months later my husband and I ventured to Cuba where we joined part of the *Catching Faith* movie team for a small film tour.

While there I was invited to teach the *Elijah Project* mentors something new. I created six activities and called them *The Next Season*, later to be called *A New Season*. Teaching in Latin America is an adventure. The experience is very organic. The day I taught our classroom lost power, the class began late, and the entire experience felt chaotic. To make it more complicated, my teaching was translated from English to Spanish which added a unique spin on presenting brand new material.

At the close of the retreat, a session was scheduled for participants to provide feedback. We taught well into the night and decided to get some rest and reconvene over breakfast. When the ladies arrived for breakfast the dining room was closed. While we waited for the kitchen crew to finish preparing our food the group sang and prayed. Once the meal began our time was even more limited than expected so our facilitator, Ingrid, instructed the women to give me three words from their experience. The ladies' words felt like pellets from a gun, pinging off my mind. I wrote feverishly while trying to make eye contact and express my gratitude for each comment. Toward the end a woman named Yudalis grabbed my hand, looked intently into my eyes, and said: *Elijah Project 1 is healing. Elijah Project 2 is growth, and Elijah Project 3 is legacy*. Like a scene in a movie my mind raced back in time to driving through the mountains in Montana then instantaneously caught up and collided with this mountain top retreat in Cuba. I knew God had spoken.

As I began writing I wracked my brain about how to represent the growth process of *The Elijah Project 2, A New Season*. I explored the metamorphosis of a caterpillar into a butterfly but the rebirth process didn't adequately capture the stage of death. The heroine's journey was also good but it required too much detail. The image that best captured my imagination was the life cycle of a leaf. The process that a leaf travels from bud to becoming cut off from its life source and being brittle provided the framework I was seeking. It also flowed perfectly with the four seasons.

God created all of life with a word. His authority, presence, and divinity set the world into orbit. The way that God brought life and order into existence transcends a moment in time. It provides a pattern for living today. Life experience begins with a dream. The dream is nurtured and develops until it reaches a critical mass and is birthed. If you spend time talking with children you can hear the expectancy and hope in their stories. Unfortunately, some time after a dream is birthed a cloud of judgment, failure, and/or criticism descends upon the little sprout. The dream may not be fully formed or spoken before something comes to attack. Many times our words are only half uttered before the spark is crushed.

We all know what it is like to encounter a dream killer. In fact we may be so pragmatic or practical that we are the dream killer ourselves. The dream may have made it out into the air without defeat but there is often a point in which the fun vision collides with a barrier or obstacle and the dream is abandoned or aborted. If the dreamer finds the strength to fight, over time negativity can lead to disillusionment causing the dream to wither, lose steam, and finally die. When the dream doesn't lead to what we hope for or expect the dreamer experiences a death.

This can be death of a spoken dream, the death of a business or ministry, the death of a relationship, or the physical death of a person. This process can feel so discouraging that it causes one not to ever want to reach for a new dream again. Satan is a dream killer. He uses shame to strip us of the power of possibility. God is the beautiful origin of a dream. With God there is always a process, a rebirth. He brings beauty from ashes. He is always in the process of redeeming—bringing life from death.

Hope is a divine gift. Throughout the Old Testament there are stories of families who were given dreams from God, then there were one or many crises and times of waning hope before the dream that God planted was fulfilled. This pattern continues today. We will birth a million little dreams in life and mourn an equal amount of little deaths.

The Elijah Project 2, A New Season will chronicle the experiences from recent seasons in my life and will use the historical figure, Queen Jezebel, as my foil. The experiences, misadventures, and tragedy of the rulers of the Northern Kingdom of Israel will serve as illustration for the power of family patterns, abuse, and trauma. Jezebel's story is quite remarkable and there is much to learn from it. While my story is not as influential or tragic, there are many life experiences and lessons from my journey that are both difficult and amazing.

This book will share the joys and sorrows of life, forging a path through some seasons in my story while following the story of Jezebel who goes down in history as the most wicked woman. Her name is synonymous with sultry, adulterous, conniving behavior. I find her fascinating because although we all suffer moments when the ugly leaks out, not many of us end up wielding our power in such destructive ways. I experience Jezebel moments even as I am striving not to live a Jezebel life. Within these pages we will also consider Eve and the tree that is the pan-ultimate part of her story.

This book is for everyone who has lived a little, because if you have lived then you have been wounded. As a little girl I played in the backyard of our house. I rode a big wheel and made forts in the woods. I fell down a lot, and got scraped up when crawling through brush. My knees have the scars to prove it. As I've grown up my scars have faded. There are few marks that you can still see 40 years after they happened. I've also been wounded by sharp words, disappointment, and pure evil. As an adult my wounds are more than scabbed knees; they have resulted in ruptured dreams. These wounds rest on the inside. As we go step by step through the seasons, the process will provide an opportunity for each of us to re-imagine some of the broken dreams from our lives.

Introduction

    I love movies. When we were first married my husband and I lived in Louisville, Kentucky. Within walking distance of our home there was a small movie house called The Baxter Avenue Theater that showed independent movies at a reduced price. We would make a goal of watching all the Academy Award nominated films before the award show. When I was young I loved the artsy movies that depicted the grit of life. As I matured and my professional social work and ministry life became more complex, I no longer needed the movies to show me the difficult side of life. I became intimately aware of how difficult life could be after spending my day listening to painful stories of trauma and loss.

    However, my love of movies has continued. Now I enjoy animated movies, musicals, and well-written uplifting stories that follow a sequential path. I appreciate a clear good guy and bad guy—a hero's journey that follows a path. It starts at the beginning, then there is a disturbance, a threshold, next we meet a mentor or helper right before a great temptation, which leads to an abyss—death and rebirth. As our hero transitions he transforms through a surrender and experiences an enlightenment. He is empowered to return on the journey and assimilates all he has learned. The hero's journey is a proven method of storytelling and the reason it works is because it is true in real life.

    Almost as much as I love movies, I love the container store. I love the multi-sized baskets, bins, and totes. Sometimes I wish I could fit my life experiences into neat boxes. I would love to order my emotions into color coded bins. But my feelings connected to my life's journey aren't linear. There are no neat boxes to check off life experiences like illness, loss, and death. And worse, we encounter many of these difficult experiences multiple times.

    While emotions are cyclical, the life cycle is linear. C.S. Lewis said it well:

You can't go back and change the beginning, but you can start where you are and change the ending.

Life experiences can move emotions backward and forward, up and down, and leave them in a jumbled mess. At some point the feelings stop matching the size of the containers, getting jostled, out of order, mixed up, and brimming over the top of the plastic seal lids.

Gifts for the Journey

This journey will require some tools. C.S. Lewis' famous character, Father Christmas from *The Chronicles of Narnia*, gave Peter, Susan, and Lucy items of value as they moved toward the Great Battle between Aslan and the White Witch. Father Christmas gave each child mysterious presents. While the children appreciated the gifts, they did not value them until the gifts were needed. When the wise men came to visit Jesus they also brought gifts: gold, frankincense, and myrrh. The wise men presented Jesus with gifts to show Him honor and respect. These were rare and expensive items in ancient times. As we embark on our journey, I believe the gifts that the wise men gave Jesus are valuable for us. These gifts are powerful metaphorical tools to allow God to take care of us on this journey.

Jesus was presented with myrrh. Myrrh is found inside special trees called the commiphora. The myrrh gum is a resin. When people harvest myrrh we wound the tree repeatedly to bleed it of its gum. The resin bleeds through the bark and coagulates to become myrrh gum. Myrrh was and is used as an antiseptic and a healing salve that may be applied to abrasions. It is a common ingredient in tooth powders because it helps ease pain. Myrrh is a gift from God to bring relief to your pain as you remember the autumn experiences that lead to winter.

Jesus was presented with frankincense. Frankincense is another resin that is harvested through tapping a tree. The tree is tapped two to three times a year and the final tap produces the best tears with the highest aromatic content. The sap is turned into anointing oil and used by churches around the world. The resin is a result of the trees' tears. God promises that He holds our tears as precious, preserving each one in a bottle until the time of His return. The frankincense oil will anoint you for your journey.

And Jesus was presented with gold. Gold is a precious metal valued around the world. Gold is weighty, it is valuable, and it is bright. The color of gold reflects the sun making it eye catching. Gold is a royal color. It is used in the United States as a measure of wealth. The gold standard is the measure in which currency is valued. God has crowned us His daughters and sons, princesses and princes of His Kingdom. Our stories are more precious than gold.

Jesus generously shares His gifts with us. He anoints us with oil, offers us antiseptic for our wounds, and crowns us with gold. King Solomon guided:

Timely advice is lovely,
 like golden apples in a silver basket.
To one who listens, valid criticism
 is like a gold earring or other gold jewelry.
 – *Proverbs 25:11-12 NLT*

Understanding the History

The stories found in this book are a combination of ancient and current. They are a mix between the heroines of the Bible and my personal story. God set the world in motion eons ago. Jezebel's story took place in the 9th century BC. My story is set in the 21st century AD. Understanding the difference between life in the modern age and life in Biblical times is very helpful.

God's divine order positioned Him as King over His people. It was never part of God's plan for Israel to have an earthly monarch. God desired to be the Israelite King and One True Ruler. God knew what the crown would do to His people and it was not part of His perfect plan.

The Hebrew people were set apart with a different form of governance than the nations that surrounded them. Israel experienced an Age of Judges. The judges lead the people in word and deed. They not only made judgments and offered wisdom to guide the people, they also lead the Hebrew army into battle. Samuel was a prophet during this time. His grown sons acted in the role of judges and made very poor decisions.

The people became disgruntled with Samuel's sons and demanded a king. They specifically *wanted to be like all the other nations—and have a king*. Samuel brought a word from the Lord about the dangers of a king's rule. In fact he listed all the reasons that God's way was better for the people than a monarchy. Despite the powerful word of the Lord, the people demanded a king and Samuel with God's guidance, anointed Saul as the first King of Israel. The first three kings charged to lead the Hebrew people were Saul, David, and Solomon. Although there were many issues with King Saul and King David, it was King Solomon who first married foreign women and invited their religious practices into the Israelite culture. With the acts of Solomon, Samuel's prophesy was fulfilled.

The religious practices of the people became more diverse and worship of the One True God was challenged. After Solomon's son succeeded him as king, the Israelites were divided into the Northern and Southern Kingdoms. Under David the Southern Kingdom experienced peace. But the Northern Kingdom was riddled with wars and distress. There were many wicked rulers; King Jeroboam was one noteworthy. He sanctioned the worship of many gods.

Omri was a very popular military leader and formed an uprising to become king of the Northern Kingdom. He was politically progressive moving the temple to the land on the hillside of Samaria that he bought. This decision made worship more accessible but it effectively stopped the Israelites' annual pilgrimages to Jerusalem. He welcomed worship of the Canaanite gods. He increased foreign trade by offering accessible worship venues for traders to worship their gods. Omri's leadership ushered in 50 years of peace. This was the longest consecutive time of peace since the division of the Northern and Southern Kingdoms. But the political brilliance brought ugly unintended consequences for God's people.

Ahab was Omri's son. The Bible specifies that *Omri did more to anger the God of Abraham, Isaac and Jacob then Jeroboam. And later the Bible notes that Ahab did worse things than even his father, as urged on by his wife Jezebel*. Under Ahab's rule the kingdom persecuted God's priests, making worship of the One True God difficult and dangerous. Simultaneously Ahab and Jezebel sanctioned the worship of Baal and Asherah directly in the temple. It is easy to judge Ahab and Jezebel for their debased way of life. But as we will discover, Jezebel was groomed for her role as queen. She was prepared for her job from birth. Just as family mores that existed for generations prepare us to fit into a family history, Jezebel was born into a royal culture that encouraged idolatrous worship. Jezebel fits into a greater story that the people of God should be aware of and cautious within.

The history of Israel—the transition from judges to kings, the split in the kingdom, the change of direction from God to Baal worship—all serve as a powerful warning. It is important to understand the pattern in order to avoid the pitfalls of the Hebrew people. It is equally important to understand our own family patterns in order to take steps toward worship of the One True God rather than stepping away.

How My History Fits Into the Story

Today is just another ordinary day in the extraordinary life of the Polnaszek's. This is a famous line my husband utters whenever our family has an incredible life experience.

My life has mirrored the story of Biblical prophet Elijah. Even as I write those words it evokes awe and wonder at the God I serve. It all started when I found myself desperately in need of a broom tree. Only at that time in my life, I didn't even know what a broom tree was. All I knew was that I felt alone and disillusioned, wondering *if this was all life really was?* At the time I had just sent our youngest daughter to all-day preschool. My entire adult life all I had ever wanted was to be a wife and mother. After 15 years of marriage and raising three kids through diapers, sleepless nights, and their first day of school, I felt purposeless. I was a dedicated pastor's wife and ministry leader. I felt disillusioned and my church wounds hurt the most. In the middle of a Bible study I heard Elijah's cry to God: *Let me go and be with my ancestors.* And then I read how God sent an angel to care for him under the broom tree. The broom tree was the image of a safe place that I desperately needed and wanted. I recognized that I needed rest. The broom tree image was so compelling that I wrote a book and workbook about it: *The Elijah Project: My Protector, My Provider.*

Looking back the next part of my journey started under the broom tree. I had lived my life striving, achieving, and pushing. While these are not bad attributes, I had a tendency to find myself on a hamster wheel—spinning around and around, pressing so hard that I missed the moments. I was striving so hard for the perfect memory or vacation that not only did I not enjoy it, neither did anyone else in my family. My behavior caused the people I loved to not feel good enough. The broom tree radically changed the course of my life and my family's future.

The tree in the middle of the wilderness represented holy permission to rest. It was God's sovereign plan that fell over me and turned negativity into positivity. He turned my striving into enjoying and gasping into breathing. I carry the broom tree image with me into every day—a symbol of God's provision and protection.

The tree from Elijah's story is a broom tree. It is a shrub found in arid climates. Its twisty bark is low to the ground with deep roots that store water to nourish it during the harsh daylight hours. The hot sun heats up its roots during the day so that the ground stays warm through the night. Elijah found warmth and protection under its branches at night.

I live in Wisconsin. There are no broom trees here. My tree of choice is an oak. Oak trees can live upwards to one thousand years. The life of an oak tree begins with one single seed found in one single acorn. The seed of an acorn germinates and produces a tap root. The tap root takes hold of the soil channeling deep into the ground and a sapling pushes upward through the ground. If all goes well this sapling grows into a mature tree. While the tree lives a long lifetime its leaves have an annual life cycle, transitioning with the seasons: spring, summer, fall, and winter.

Each leaf has a one year lifespan. Spring brings a bud, a small green knob that will burst into summer as a leaf. In fall the tree will stop nourishing the leaf causing its color to change from green to red, orange, or yellow. The process of cutting off nourishment to the leaf is called scarring. As the temperature drops the tree is triggered to end its food supply to the leaf. Once the leaf has drained every last bit of nutrients from its branch it turns brown and becomes brittle. The most fascinating part of an oak leaf's journey is the end. It is winter now and the tree has stopped feeding the leaf which is brown, brittle, and for all intents and purposes dead. But the stem is so securely attached to its branch, that it often will not let go until spring. The stem finally loses its grip when the new bud underneath pushes through in search of sunlight. The bud dislodges the dead leaf from its perch and the dead leaf wafts to the ground. The journey of the leaf provides a beautiful framework for the life cycle of a dream.

Humans are given the initial divine spark at the start of life. Then we are given many little sparks or dreams during our lifetimes. While each person has one life similar to the tree, our dreams traverse multiple seasons similar to that of the leaf. Human life endeavors do not progress people through the time frame as neatly as the leaf does, but the analogy can be helpful as a guide. We emotionally experience spring, summer, fall, and winter a few times over in our life. Human life is complex and many dreams can occur at the same time. So, depending on what stage the dream is in, a person may experience multiple seasons at the same time.

God created life to be cyclical, a circle, not a strict linear trajectory. Human beings are created in the image of God which is different and distinct from the plants and animals. The simplicity of the life cycle of a leaf offers a metaphor for personal human growth over time.

Finding a Path for the Journey

This book has a flow intended to help the reader learn, grow, and process. It is divided into the four seasons. For each season there is a section including my story, Jezebel's story, an explanation of the season, and finally an activity that allows the reader to process his or her own story in context to the topic of the section.

As we explore our own family trees it is vitally important to note both good and bad family traits. There will be many things that are a gifts to the next generation but unlike Jezebel let's be open to examining the negative family patterns and finding the courage to change them.

God's ways are not our ways and His instructions can feel uncomfortable and challenging. But His ways are the best ways. Solomon offers invaluable wisdom in *Proverbs*. The way of living that he outlines will lead to pleasure in the eyes of Lord, but the steps are not easy. In fact even though the words came from Solomon he did not always heed them and his own lust was his downfall.

Life begins with promise, expectation, and hope. But all life will come to an end on this side of heaven. Humans wrestle with the limits of our humanity and we have since the beginning of time. We struggle with death because the original design was to be alive with God forever. Eve was seduced by the idea that she could be like God and see good and evil. The act of eating the forbidden fruit set humanity into constant struggle with life and death.

This book will use the seasons as a guide for the cycle of life. The 4 Ds is a framework for this seasons work. The 4 Ds are described like this: The ***Dream*** stage in when something is new. Whether it is the discovery of a mutual attraction or the excitement of a new job this is a time full of hope and promise. The ***Development*** phase is when an idea, experience, or relationship begins to grow. We develop a new understanding and then master the tasks related to our business or experience. The growth eventually hits a barrier and we experience ***Disillusionment***. The stage between development and death is when the work becomes hard; we reach the limit of what we know, we experience criticism, and failure occurs. This is the point in a friendship when you may realize the faults or negative attributes of another. This is when the honeymoon period at your job ends and it can lead to a sense of despondency. This is the point when all hope is lost.

Often despondency is accompanied by feelings of melancholy. This is the state of being pensive or sad. It is the feeling that occurs when the mind begins to embrace the disappointment and loss. Finally the losses mount and there is ***Death***. It is the pan-ultimate loss. Death is the end of a matter and it is accompanied by suffocating sadness. It can feel like grief settles into your bones and just won't leave. Some people describe it like a dark cloud that moves directly overhead and never leaves.

Sometimes it is helpful to be reminded that the cycle of life is normal. From the inception of a dream, loss is lingering out there. The end can take many forms. Death of a person is the most final but individuals also grieve dreams for a career, children, the accumulation of wealth, health, and much more. The seasons and the 4 Ds fit like this:

Spring – Dream

Summer – Development

Fall – Disillusionment

Winter – Death.

Because life is not easily organized with boxes, bins, and containers various dreams or life stages may be at different points of the 4 Ds continuum at the same time. Real life does not organize as neatly as we may desire. While these illustrations will fail at some point, they serve as a way to organize our ideas and experience.

M.S. Lowndes poem, *The Seasons Of Life* summarizes these concepts well. My favorite lines from the poem are:

It is but for a season,
That we are in this place.
We need not sit and question it,
Just receive His loving grace.

There is a sense of wonder with God's divine timing and the beautiful promise of His presence. While questioning can sometimes feel fruitless, processing is important. Gather up your gifts from Jesus and enter into the journey prayerfully, wrapping yourself is His loving grace.

A Prayer to Guide the Journey

Reinhold Niebuhr is not a household name, yet his influence has shaped a generation of people seeking recovery from addiction. Historian Arthur Schlesinger, Jr., described Niebuhr as "the most influential American theologian of the 20th century" and *Time Magazine* posthumously called Niebuhr "the greatest Protestant theologian in

America since Jonathan Edwards." He left his fingerprints on the most successful recovery work in our country when he wrote *The Serenity Prayer*. Today Alcoholic Anonymous groups routinely quote the beginning of his prayer. I find the depth of his theology in the later stanzas that are lesser known. I encourage you to use this prayer to ground your self-exploration and healing.

The Serenity Prayer

God grant me the serenity
To accept the things I cannot change;
Courage to change the things I can;
And wisdom to know the difference.

Living one day at a time;
Enjoying one moment at a time;
Accepting hardships as the pathway to peace;
Taking, as He did, this sinful world
As it is, not as I would have it;
Trusting that He will make all things right
If I surrender to His Will;
So that I may be reasonably happy in this life
And supremely happy with Him
Forever and ever in the next.

Amen.

(prayer attributed to Reinhold Niebuhr, 1892-1971)

Spring: Dream

*Sometimes the dreams that come true are the dreams
you never knew you had.*
– anonymous

*He had a dream in which he saw a stairway resting on the earth, with
its top reaching to heaven, and the angels of God were ascending and
descending on it.*
– Genesis 28:12

*In the last days, God says,
I will pour out my spirit on all people.
Your sons and daughters will prophesy,
your young men will see visions,
your old men will dream dreams.*
– Acts 2.17

Chapter 1:

We're Making a Movie

The day was warm and bright. People bustled about in a unique room, designed to embrace the outdoors behind the safety and warmth of glass. The repurposed clear-pane garage doors filled the room with light. A stainless steel table preserved from a '50s diner was being set, not with dishes but with art supplies. As I took each glass jar out of my supply box, I could feel in my stomach the flutter of expectancy and disbelief. The markers, colored pencils, and highlighters which had been used time and time again to encourage creativity, growth, and healing for women studying *The Elijah Project* were now props. YES, props for a real life movie.

The rest of that day I watched the words our writing team had scripted morph into life as five actresses portrayed the real life ladies small group I had hosted on Thursdays for so many years. The movie would tell the fictional story of Alexa Taylor's spiritual transformation come to life through her work with *The Elijah Project*.

The actress, Lizz Carter, ushered in mystery and excitement when she opened the box revealing the brand new study the women would complete. As the white lid was lifted the cover of *The Elijah Project* workbook was revealed. My heart skipped a beat as the workbook I had written was presented. This book, complete with the activities that so many women had shared and perfected, and the pages that my friend Renee Wurzer had painstakingly poured over to edit, were now captured on film. This was a plan for my life that I had not ever imagined. And standing in the wings of the set, it was becoming reality.

In the script, the woman leading the small group was named Jael. She delivered her lines with anticipation and passion, sharing a snippet paraphrasing the Bible story in *1 Kings* and then gave directions for her group to complete the activity. In the world of movie making the scenes are shot multiple times. So by the end of the day the scene was seared in my brain. The experience felt momentous, weighty, and holy. Little did I know what those scenes would bring when they were received by the world.

Sometime Later

God broke through again. I left church early, taking our daughter to the high school for a show choir practice. When I arrived home our house was empty and I took the dog for a walk. When I returned our house was a buzz of activity with church folks dishing up chili and getting ready to watch the noon football game. I bustled into the house. My husband called out over his shoulder: *Andrea, Judy wants to talk to you about your next movie.* I sat down next to her and Judy began to ask me questions about a script we had just finished, *Catching Faith 2*. She inquired about timelines and what kind of investment we needed. I answered each question in stride, not really reading in, just offering the information I knew about the process. As the conversation continued, the thought went through my mind: *I wonder if she has a rich uncle or brother who might want to invest?* The fleeting thought came and went. The more I talked the more excited I became about filming the reprise to our story. I was excited to share the next season. And I was invested to see the movie made in our neck of the woods.

And then it came. Judy looked at me and said: *God told me this weekend that I am supposed to invest in your movie.* I looked intently into her eyes, with the words hanging in the air. I thought: *No, couldn't be... I was just talking, sharing. This wasn't a pitch, we were just chatting.* I don't remember what I said next but I remember asking if we could pray about it. I do remember saying: *Judy, our friendship is more important than money. I don't want anything to come between us.* She gently shook her head, grabbed my hands and we began to pray. When we opened our eyes, I half expected the offer to be rescinded. But instead Judy said: *Andrea, God told me to do this and I have to obey Him.* My heart said: *How can I argue with that?* My flesh was astounded by God's presence.

My friend Judy, a woman of faith who has dedicated her life to run group homes for mentally challenged men, now a widow, had just offered her savings to invest in our movie. The gravity of that moment will stick with me. It felt like Jesus' story of the woman who gave her only coin as an offering to Him. The entire time I was engaged in a conversation with my friend, I was actually speaking with what the movie biz calls *first money in*.

This provision was the beginning of a string of blessings that led me to my own personal next season. The presence of God was unmistakable and this time Judy was my angel. She looked at me and said: *Andrea, you need to let me bless you in this way.*

I accepted the blessing and received a sign that day—God is truly the protector and provider. This was the spring and all the seasons were to follow.

Chapter 2:

Tyrian Purple

The sun shone bright above the castle. There was a bustle about the kingdom—something new was afoot. The place named after the Greek word for purple, was known for tyrian powder. A message was being passed from servant to servant. Once outside the doors of the castle shopkeepers shook their heads as the request was made known. They would sheepishly point to the end of the road. There sat a tent made of ornately decorated Arabian rugs. One guard held up the corner as the other entered the eerie enclosure. The incense wafted and filled his nostrils. Just two words: *Tyrian purple?* A wrinkled hand pressed a vial into the rough palace guard's fist. With a swift movement the rug fell, kicking up dust beneath its tassels, and the guards were gone.

The journey continued back to the castle where the vial was passed to a gentle looking woman who emptied the precious contents into a large iron cauldron. She patiently stirred as thick purple bubbles hovered over the giant pot. An upstairs chamber was filled with whispers broken by screams. Cool clothes were pressed on a woman's forehead while quiet directions were given at the bedside. The woman would gasp and sputter and bellow again. It would not be long now.

Out of the cauldron came a square of soft purple fabric. The woman hung it up on a coarse rope. Large droplets of thick amaranth colored liquid collected dying the dirt floor beneath. Upstairs another woman with great skill guided and pulled a small mass of skin and blood from its dark safe womb. A strong cry collided with the cold callous walls of the royal room.

Blood stained the floor beneath the birthing table, the red molecules stacking up in a pile. No one seemed to notice the blood. No one noticed the dye. The purple blanket was folded and sent upstairs—both floors left stained, the red representing sacrifice, the purple representing royalty, all for a greater cause. She is here. A princess is born. The midwife inspected the tiny human and declared: *She is perfect, just beautiful.* The doors were unlocked and the servant barged through with a cloth made of the most vivid indigo. The queen wrapped her daughter tightly in the silk fibers.

Soon, the king entered. He picked up the royal package and gazing at the precious face he declared for all to hear: *Daughter of Baal. She will carry on our traditions. She will be known throughout the land not just for her beauty but also for her wit.*

Every day was a new day. There was so much promise, so much hope, so much to accomplish. She will be trained to someday be the queen.

Sometime Later

She moved through the palace with ease. She may be a newcomer but her role was well practiced. With a toss of her perfectly coiffed hair and bat of her made up lashes onlookers noticed her. She was captivating and some might say intoxicating. She had the best of perfumes doused on her body and the scents wafted behind her as she glided through the room. She was beautiful and cunning. Only if you had the guts to make eye contact would you notice the dull disconnect behind her eyes. Her presence and poise allowed her to persuade the only one more powerful than she.

Omri had set the stage years before. He had bought Samaria and moved the capital there. He had stopped the pilgrimage to Jerusalem and brought peace in the kingdom. These advancements had set the stage perfectly for his daughter-in-law. The people of the Northern Kingdom had more to learn from their new Queen Jezebel. Omri had ushered in a sense of tolerance that made the region ripe for her influence. She had convinced her king that it was only right to have fair representation in the temple. She was going to show everyone the ways of her land.

Jezebel persuaded her husband, Ahab, to build two temples: one in Samaria to honor the sun god and another in Jezreel. Such forward thinking allowed the worship of all Canaanite gods in the Hebrew temples. She was the mastermind behind the Asherah poles and the temple of Baal. Always perfectly put together from head to toe, wearing those foreign fashions, she was wielding her power from morning until night. This indeed is what she was made for. A new queen is in charge and change is coming.

Chapter 3:

Budding

  Spring is quite literally the time for birth or rebirth. The world is waking up. The sun hangs in the sky longer. The air is getting warmer. Spring is hopeful, captivating, and urgent. A small green bud emerges from its lofty perch. It wriggles and grows toward the sliver of light. It hears crackles as if crisp breaks are happening. It presses forward knocking a brittle bit of foliage out of its way. One more push and the green plant is flooded by light and warm busy life-filled air. The small shell of its former self hangs in the sky dropping to its inevitable death.

  Springtime in life is birth: new life, new dreams, and hope.

  The divine breath of God was breathed into human beings and one way it manifests itself is through stages of life. The springtime of life is birth and early childhood, which is infancy to age five. Science confirms that social, emotional, and physical development begins before a baby enters the world. In utero a baby can feel music, experience uncomfortable emotions, and sense stress. While spring is a time of hope, brokenness still exists and often the womb is not safe from trauma. During early childhood children begin to develop an understanding of themselves and the world around them. Every day is a new day full of hope and the opportunity for dreams to come true.

  Jezebel had the world at her feet. She was a princess with all her kingdom had to offer at her disposal. Little girls everywhere dreamed of changing places with her. She had food, a warm bed, and beautiful clothes. From the outside she had the dream life.

  I was given the gift of being a stay-at-home mother. Many people looked in on my life and envied my opportunity to stay home. When our daughter was born, our son was two and a half and he loved Thomas the Tank Engine. Every morning we would get up and set up his train tracks. He would move his trains on the track and tell stories. Then we would eat a snack, watch a Thomas the Tank Engine VHS movie, and get back down on the floor to play. After lunch he took a nap and when he woke up we played trains until it was time for me to make dinner. The only diversion to this plan was nursing the baby, changing her diapers, or taking a walk. It was like the movie *Groundhog Day* for parenting. In the movie *Groundhog Day*, Bill Murray's character woke up to re-experience the same day over and over again until he figured out how to change his bad patterns.

Repetition is vitally important for learning, creating safety, and the healthy development of children. As a parent of young children it can feel mundane and boring. At the time I wondered if our Thomas the Tank Engine season would ever end. Today the box of wooden train tracks and colorful train engines sits in my living room, only used when families with young children come to visit. The season did end and looking back what waned on in the present seems like a moment in the past.

Sometimes my tendency is to rush out of a season because it is uncomfortable. As I grow older I realize that there is something special about every season and it is important to treasure it in the moment because it may not be part of the next season. I found raising preschoolers a bit mind numbing. I really didn't appreciate the season for all that it was. My husband was our breadwinner. This allowed me to take walks, read books, and have my love tank filled by hours of hugs and cuddling. During my season of raising teenagers I find myself looking back to the hours of reading under the covers during snow storms. I realized this was beyond a gift, it was an extraordinary blessing.

Spring is the time of dreams. It is an opportunity to experience the power of imagination. Springtime in my children's lives was important and required a valuable deposit that I am so thankful I could give them. Springtime in my parenting was full of wonder and joy, questions and worries. Sometimes I wish I could return to the innocence of early parenting and other times I am grateful for the wisdom gained in 18 years of motherhood.

Activity A: The Season of Spring

Spring DREAM – DELIGHT – HOPE

Use the tree to create what Spring looks like in your life.
- What experience marked this time in your life?
- Use color, images, and words to describe what you felt during this season.
- Identify the experience, time, date, or circumstance of the season.

Reflect:

And God said, "Let there be lights in the vault of the sky to separate the day from the night, and let them serve as signs to mark sacred times, and days and years."
– Genesis 1:14

Process:

Take a look at your tree. What do you feel when it is Spring in your story?

Pray:

God,

Thank you for the gift of hope. I often long for the light and life of springtime. Thank you for a season to help me reflect on new birth. Amen

Summer: Development

Strength and growth come only through continuous effort and struggle.
– Napoleon Hill

I made you grow like a plant of the field. You grew and developed and entered puberty…
– Ezekiel 16:7

The Lord GOD made all kinds of trees grow out of the ground—trees that were pleasing to the eye and good for food. In the middle of the garden were the tree of life and the tree of the knowledge of good and evil.
– Genesis 2:9

Chapter 4:

We Made a Movie

The longest part of making a movie comes after the filming stops. After the actors fly home, the props are put away, and the locations return to their previous roles, a team of skilled editors painstakingly edit, sound design, and color correct the captured footage. For *Catching Faith* this process was spearheaded by my brother-in-law. After the long days, creative connections, and fun energy of being on set, post-production is like the air being let out of a balloon. Team members often experience a little let down after filming. Suddenly we find ourselves back in the day-to-day of life without evidence of what we have done. There is no painting to look at or book to read. It is just over.

One day months after filming we received an uncut version of the film. I was so excited to see the story played out. My husband and I set up our computer, sat on the couch, and watched. This was my first experience with a movie before color correction and sound design. I remember experiencing a worse let down than the end of filming. There was a distinct sense *of this is it?* In several conversations with my sister and brother-in-law we received reassurance; this was the rough cut of the story and once a score was added the movie would have a better feel. This was all the development, the growth of the process.

The movie's working title was *The Elijah Project* inspired by the book of the same name. Test audiences and an executive producer gave insight: audiences imagined a guy in a robe with a long white beard and not a family film. So, as the finished product came within sight a new name emerged; *Catching Faith* was a bonafide film. The movie was purchased by Image Entertainment and set to be released in August.

Plans were made and permission given to host a premiere at our local Micon Cinemas in the hometown of the film—Chippewa Falls. That night was truly enchanted. A limo picked up the stars, the crew and our dearest supporters. We arrived to a red carpet and a sell-out crowd unlike anything I could have hoped for or imagined. Pictures, accolades, congratulations. Joined by my family and lifelong friends who lived all over the country, my heart was bigger than I could have ever dreamed. Our little experiment to represent Christian women with real life struggle was met with thunderous applause.

Sometime Later

I parked and walked into our local big box store. The greeter smiled and welcomed me. I walked directly to the back of the store where a half dozen televisions mounted to the wall displayed a sundry of mainstream Hollywood movies. My eyes glanced up and then down to a section of DVDs labeled New Releases. Scanning the movie titles I saw the now familiar picture of a football player kneeling and the title: *Catching Faith*. Nothing can really prepare you for the feeling of standing anonymously in the aisle of Wal-Mart looking at the cover art of a movie you contributed to. Hundreds of people would shop in that store that day. No one knew who I was. But I had a once-in-a-lifetime moment seeing my movie on the store shelf.

And then the Facebook pictures began to roll in from cities all over the United States with testimonies of people who had bought the movie and been moved by the story. In October of 2015 *Catching Faith* was put on Netflix. This is when the testimonies changed from *The movie spoke to me* to *I bought The Elijah Project workbook and it did amazing things in my life.*

One of the women who contacted me was Ingrid Duarte. She lived in Ocala, Florida. She called to share that she had led a small group of women from her church through *The Elijah Project*. She now wondered if she could translate the workbook into Spanish for a ministry she led in Cuba. I was sitting on the landing at the top of the steps in my house. The kitchen was full of Saturday morning chaos as my husband made pancakes and my girls sang Broadway show tunes. I didn't think much about the request. I didn't hesitate or consult with anyone; I just said yes and asked for her email address. Ingrid later shared that she was shocked to speak with the author of the book and was even more shocked that the author would say *yes* and almost immediately send the word document to a woman she did not know.

Catching Faith continued to perform well and *The Elijah Project* ministry expanded. Ingrid translated the workbook and we printed 25 copies for her to take to Cuba. The night before she left the United States, Ingrid sent a picture of her luggage. There were pink *Proyecto de Elias* t-shirts, workbooks, and a sundry of craft supplies including pipe cleaners and colored pencils just like the ones that had adorned the table when we filmed the ladies small group scene many months before. Four days later I received a text with a 20-second video greeting from 25 Cuban women thanking me for *The Elijah Project*. With the picture seared in my mind, I walked along the bike trail behind my home, watching our dog romp on the grass. I shared the story with my husband and choking back tears Perry said: *I think something BIG is happening.*

Chapter 5:

Growing Up Royal

Something big was happening. She shuffled behind desperately trying to make her three little steps equal his one giant step. He would stop and point—this is Asherah, the goddess of fertility. She is the author of our life. We must keep her happy so that our kingdom flourishes. It was difficult not to notice the tears of the peasant as she stood next to the statue and palace guards grabbed her baby. But this man with his commanding voice and kind eyes called her to something more; he challenged her to a place in his kingdom and in the world. It didn't need to make sense; she just needed to obey.

Soon it will be your turn little Jezi. The priests will prepare you for your job as a princess of Phoenicia, he said. She wondered what that meant but trusted her father implicitly as he strode with pride and respect explaining the many rituals their family had honored for generations.

There was an unspoken message that she received clearly from the time she had understood her father's words—the sacrifice is worth it, the tears and pain will make you stronger. You will be my great heiress and in order to fulfill that role, sacrifices must be made. Today she got to go to work with her dad and that was all that mattered. As they walked the palace workers bowed their heads and motioned with signs of respect. She would nod back and sometimes receive a wink.

Back in her quarters, a small girl with kind eyes helped her disrobe. Jasmine was her name and she was the daughter of Jezi's maidservant Jasmine coaxed Jezi's arm out of her dress while whispering: *What was it like?*

Jezi bubbled back: *It was awesome! Did you know that one day I will rule over all the land? I will be in charge of appeasing the gods. I will be making the ritual sacrifices. One day I'll be queen.*

Jasmine's eyes widened. She could only imagine the life of a princess, though she saw it firsthand. She made it happen but she could only imagine what it felt like to wear dresses like this one, eat decadent food until her belly was full, and walk in the footsteps of the king. She also knew there was something hollow in the traditions of the gods. There was something wanting in the worship of Asherah. And there was something distinctly different about her God, the Hebrew God, the God who didn't like pagan worship.

These girls would grow up together in entirely different worlds with entirely different world views. But for now they were partners, each having a job to do, and they would fulfill their destinies better together than apart.

Sometime Later

Jez! Her mom's gentle voice came from the other side of her chambers. *Do you have everything you need?* The beautiful woman with raven hair who had quietly obeyed the king's wishes had a small tear rolling down her cheek. She sniffled. The trunks were packed plus an entire box filled with small carvings and the things Jezi would need for the ritual sacrifice.

A gentle hug was invaded by the booming voice: *I am so proud of you, extending our kingdom beyond the shores. You are expanding the culture and customs of Phoenicia beyond our land. You will go down in history as a great leader.*

The hug ended. She put on her brave face as she was lifted into her chariot and triumphantly exited the kingdom as townspeople called out her name in the streets.

Sometime Even Later

Of course, dear! What else can I do for you dear? She rode by to inspect the Asherah poles. It had taken many dinners of his favorite, specially prepared beef cut from cattle only found in the hill country, fruits available out of season because each had been preserved, and the belly dancers. She hated the belly dancers. She had paid great attention to detail as she made the arrangements night after night. Servants had been flogged or fired—a small price to pay for the ear of the king. Each evening after stuffing himself silly and drinking too much wine, the timing was right. She would request one thing. First: *Could I add an Asherah pole to the rose garden?* Next: *A statue to Baal would look magnificent in the castle courtyard.* Night after night her requests became more and more bold extending beyond the palace: *How about an Asherah pole at every major intersection in the city?* Finally, the pièce de résistance: *A bronze statue of Baal with receptacles all around for worshippers to leave their offerings, right in the center of Solomon's temple... wouldn't that be perfect...* she imagined.

Her plan was complete. Although still foreign and a bit drab for her taste, the city finally looked a little more like home. She was part of making worship to her gods easy and it encouraged more foreign trade, even with the Canaanites. *They like to visit now. They can visit, trade and settle because there is a place for them to worship.* She was fulfilling her father's wish that she too would be a great leader.

Chapter 6:

Growing

The bud pushes out from the stem and becomes a full grown leaf. It is a vivid green now. Its stem is snugly attached to the branch. It is safe and securely attached. Summer is generally a happy time. There is joy in the air as flowers bloom, birds sing, and the sun waits longer and longer each day before hiding. The world seems cheerful and alive. The leaf dances in the wind. It knows where it belongs. All the leaves together are a most beautiful garment adorning the tree. The world is filled with lush shades of green. The forest is burgeoning with life and almost feels enchanted. Life teams around the leaf. Some caterpillars spin their cocoons right onto the leaf. The leaf acts as a cradle, keeping the cocoon safe until the moth is ready to be born. The leaf is a safe place. It is vibrant, nourished by the tree beneath and the sun above. Life is good.

Summer is a season for rewards, celebration, and fulfillment. In Jim Rohn's *The Art of Exceptional Living* he suggests that the seasons should be valued and protected. The summer of life is childhood and adolescence from 6 to 20 years old. There is a sense of innocence, expectancy, and hope during these years. We should protect the summer; it is a time when we reap the benefits of all that has been planted and nurtured. There is learning, growth, and maturation. During summer there is a sense of abundant energy, the ability to try and try again. The spark of life—the dream—is now growing, developing, and expanding.

Summer for Jezebel included learning about her culture. She received tutoring and instruction about her family values and the mores of her country. She was betrothed to a prince which provided her with financial security for the future. In my youth, I received much of the same advantages as Jezebel and I attempted to provide the same things for my children. Now my children are school age. While I am in middle adulthood, they are in the summer of their lives. Their minds are being expanded by new ideas and influences. They are being challenged to try new things. My influence has shifted. I am often called *Miss Bernhardt*, a favorite second grade teacher's name. While my children are off learning to read and write, I am reading and writing again myself. New dreams are being born.

While all of this good happens during the summer period of life, challenging experiences can begin to carve out pathways in the brain reinforcing that not all people are safe. Life can be disappointing. Significant hurt exists in the world.

As a teenage girl I remember my mother saying: *Don't hurry to grow up so fast.* At the time, I didn't heed her words. She said: *Don't work so hard, you will have a job for the rest of your life.* She was right! I spent the summers of my adolescence working multiple jobs. I earned a lot of money and developed a great work ethic. But that development phase gave way to adulthood where the work never seems to end.

Now when I experience bursts of summer, I protect and savor them. Summer is a time of reaping the benefits of what you have planted and nurtured. When you get the chance celebrate the light, life, and growth that this season brings.

Activity B: The Season of Summer
Summer DEVELOPMENT – GROWTH – LIFE
Use the tree to create what Summer looks like in your life.
- What experience marked this time in your life?
- Use color, images, and word to describe what you felt during this season.
- Identify the experience, time, date, or circumstance of the season.

Reflect:

Go to the ant, you sluggard;
consider its ways and be wise!
It has no commander,
no overseer or ruler,
yet it stores its provisions in summer
and gathers its food at harvest.
– *Proverbs 6:6-8*

Process:

Take a look at your tree. What do you feel when it is Summer in your story?

Pray:

Dear Lord,

Thank you for giving me the feeling of growth, development, and thriving in my heart, mind, and soul. Amen

Fall: Disappointment

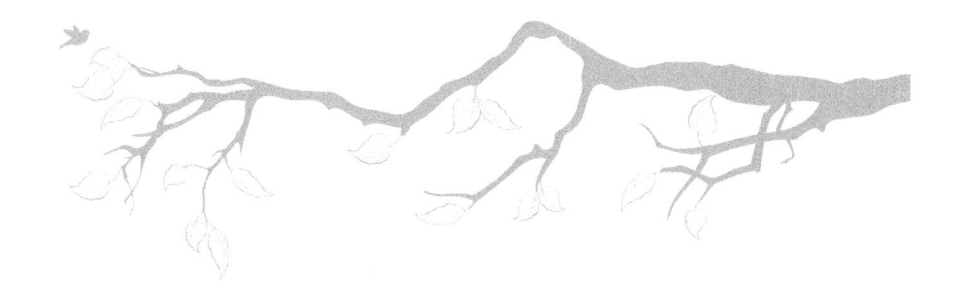

*In the beginning was the dream and the work of
disenchantment never ends.*
− Kim Stanley

*So the L*ORD *God caused the man to fall into a deep sleep;
and while he was sleeping, he took one of the man's ribs and
then closed up the place with flesh.*
− Genesis 2:21

*Now the springs of the deep and the floodgates of the heavens had been
closed, and the rain had stopped falling from the sky.*
− Genesis 8:2

Chapter 7:

Back to School

The alarm blared, it was 3 a.m. My husband attempted to ease out of bed. I lay quiet, eyes closed, but I could hear as he slipped on his work clothes, then glided down the stairs and out the door. As the glass door slid open and shut, I was all too aware of where he was going.

Things had gotten hard. After the movie, church attendance continued to plummet.

Every other week on payday it was uncertain as to whether the church offering would be enough to meet our salary. Sometimes we got a check and sometimes we did not. In October it was no longer possible to make ends meet on our bare bones salary. Out of necessity, my husband got a job working nights at UPS. He unloaded the trucks filled with holiday packages for people who had the privilege to prepare for the Christmas season this year. I'm not sure I had ever thought of Christmas preparation as a privilege but it indeed was. He came home day after day bruised and battered. After dinner he would sleep on the couch attempting to catch a little nap while the girls snuggled up on either side next to him. They missed his presence. His pride was slowly dissipating and I knew it was time.

I sat in a newly remodeled office space. A southwestern style woven rug hung on the wall. Two women entered the room. They both complimented me on my resume. One woman looked at me with a twinkle in her eye and said: *You have a lot of experience.* The other woman was warm but more distant, she said: *You can shadow me. I'm trusting you with the reputation I have grown over the past ten years of practice.* My desire to people please was activated by the weight in her words. Then, just like that, after ten years out of the full time work force, I was hired.

Things progressed slowly but it wasn't long before I was listening to, guiding, and advocating for my clients. The first year I bootstrapped back into the groove. I worked hard to understand what had changed in social work practice while I was home playing with Thomas the Tank Engine and Dora the Explorer.

In retrospect it didn't take long before I began to receive referrals in my own right. I met and served clients, building from quarter time to full time in two years. During this time I was invited to work for my sister and brother-in-law's company, Mustard Seed Entertainment.

Our team wrote, filmed, and completed a second faith-based movie: *Wish for Christmas*. This movie did two things for me. First it solidified that I really enjoyed making movies. I loved the creative energy, the vision to bring an idea from paper to life. And at the same time it reinforced a personal sense of frailty. Making movies represented a proverbial rope of sorts that had a distinct beginning and an end—a continuum with a definite point of exhaustion.

I took a three-week leave from my job to be part of making *Wish for Christmas*. I returned from the extended break on a Saturday and went back to work with my clients on Monday morning. This cycle continued for the next two years. The glamorous jaunts to Los Angeles were met with a daunting workload at home. In the midst of all that I had a growing family. I increasingly missed dinner and a new season had been ushered in where I was no longer the stay-at-home parent. I became the second one to receive the stories. I no longer signed the assignment notebook, listened to the assigned reading homework, or doled out the snack. I all too often returned home after 7 p.m., found my dinner plate covered in the microwave and collapsed next to our ten-year-old to watch 30 minutes of television before tucking her into bed.

Sometime Later

I looked around. Could it be true? While singing on Sunday it had felt like my voice echoed of the padded movie theater walls. It sounded a though I was in a cave or exhaling into a deep cavern. My home church was empty. All the familiar faces were gone. I counted 30 heads including me and the kids. What was happening? I was receiving letters from women around the world who had met God in a new and vibrant way through *The Elijah Project* and I was sitting practically alone in Fellowship—the church my husband and I had started nine years earlier. We were hanging on, but something was happening that didn't feel so good.

Erosion happens slowly. Whether it is sand at the seashore or confidence in the workplace, it is a slow gradual process. Erosion can be particularly difficult to detect within friendships. Life is busy and it often takes weeks or months for schedules to allow an intersection. At church it first was one person, then a family, and finally I was sitting in a meeting with one remaining elder couple wondering where everyone had gone. Patterns were difficult to identify. The story surrounding each new departure was different from the ones that came before. But this did not change the dull ache in my heart. People I loved, served with, and had spiritually grown with departed. As I looked around at the empty seats it felt as though they'd left without a trace.

Disenchantment mirrors disillusionment and signals the breakdown of the known into the abyss of the unknown. Somehow seeds of disappointment had been sown and began to grow. It was easier to be quiet than to speak the loss out loud.

My husband has a motto—*At some point, I am going to disappoint you. I promise you, I will let you down.* When he first started to say this, I felt like I wanted to puff up and defend that he was a good friend. His words seemed so pessimistic and self-defeating, but the older I get the more I realize how true the saying has become. Even when I have the best intentions, I can hurt or disappoint others.

The phases of most relationships include a romance, a sense of being enamored with someone else. During this time the relationship is new and fun. As the relationship grows and two people get to know each other better, differing opinions are revealed and differing world views emerge. The longer we are friends and the more time we spend together, the more opportunity there is for divergent viewpoints which can lead to hurtful things being said and disappointing decisions being made. It is natural and healthy to have expectations but when one person is not aligned with the others' thoughts and values it can lead to a contradictory choice, and a little bit of the common ground in the relationship erodes away. Jezebel and Jasmine manifest an innocent childhood friendship, one that grows more distant as their differences are exposed with age.

I have had the honor of many long-lasting friendships and wonderful relationships with my family. I realize that in these relationships we have chosen to work through the uncomfortable places of disagreement and hang in the dissonance until we find some common ground again. Unfortunately in our church family, when the dissonant dust settled, only three founding families remained.

The process of telling this story produces a lump in my throat and a seizing in my belly. Even though I found the courage to write it down, sharp emotion remains attached to it. Recounting the fall of our church and the autumn of my church planting dream is painful. As I write, I am still in autumn on this part of the dream. The remaining leaves are brown, dry, tired, and worn out. I feel dry, tired, and concerned that I don't have the energy to re-engage in new relationships.

Chapter 8:

When the Castle Can't Protect You

It was the big day. She was so excited. Not only did she have a day with her father but she was going to the most coveted place. Her handmaidens helped her put on a most beautiful magenta silk gown. They put the crown with the crystal flowers in her hair. She looked beautiful, felt beautiful, was beautiful. She floated down the palace steps to meet the king. He gave one last instruction to his assistant and then took her hand. They were off to the temple.

It had been some time since she had visited the big temple, the one that was up the mountain from the palace. She waved to the subjects as she and the king passed through town. Once up the hillside, the stone pillars seemed colder than she remembered. Men in robes, with their faces covered, bowed to her father. He approached the grand gold monument to Baal as she was ushered into a side room. It was dark and cold. They gave her something to drink and she became very sleepy.

She sits upright still not able to feel her body. She can feel each rock under the chariot. Her father gently touches her knee and she recoils in surprised fright. And then it is dark again.

The rest is a blurry dream that ends in night terror. Her head bobs and nods as her body slowly wakes. Her mind races to catch up. She glances around the room. It is familiar. It is her safe space. Jasmine is tucking the sheets into the side of her bed. She looks concerned. She is cautious. Jezi's eyes desperately communicate with her friend: *What happened? When did I get home? Where is my father?* She pushes herself up, attempting to sit upright. The familiar decor spins around her and gravity pulls her back down into her bed. She is asleep.

She opens her eyes again. This had happened before. Through foggy eyes young maidens were cleaning her up. Her beautiful dress was gone. She was wrapped in a bloody sheet. She still can't feel anything. She is numb. That haunting dream that her mother had comforted her through so many times before, maybe it wasn't a dream after all. Something was clear through the haze of her drugged-out mind; being a Phoenician princess wasn't all good.

Jasmine lifts a warm liquid to her lips. The smell is comforting, lavender, she thinks. It's easier to keep her eyes open now. She is home. From her perch she can view her armoire door open just a crack, puff of violet fabric jutting out. Jasmine is in her chambers and so are the other hand maidens. But something was different about her. She is more jumpy. She has less grace her for servants' mistakes. Her insides feel hardened. She feels desensitized, tough, and resolved.

She is overcome by a strange emotion. This feeling is the opposite of mercy. She feels violated and a violent anger accompanies it. No longer the sweet girl, she is now a determined woman. No longer will she be hurt, instead she will do the hurting. She has a job to do and she vows to do it.

Sometime Later

On what seemed like the opposite side of the world a new chariot met her. This one is different. It is adorned with dark metals, not the bright colors of her homeland. She is welcomed with the cheers of her new people. In this new land it is impossible to miss a large temple that looks nothing like the one she had left.

As she approaches the castle there stands a man. He is older, shoulders slumped, and a bit disheveled. His crown is fixed crooked on top of his wavy dark hair. A larger ominous-looking man stands beside him. When the chariot stops a voice bellows, *Ahab help her out!* A limp wrist juts out before her. *Ha,* she thinks, *this is going to be easier than I thought.* She stands up on her own, brushing away his hand and with a determined expression faces her new staff: *Take these things upstairs. I am famished. It was a long trip.* She had expected to meet a warrior king, a formidable opponent. Where is the guy who had conquered lands and expanded the kingdom's territory? Marriage is going to be easy she thought. She could already see how she would get her own way. He seemed like a spoiled brat. It became clear quickly; she had been pledged to do life with a weak-willed wuss.

Sometime Even Later
Her prophets stood before her for inspection. She looked them up and down and gave them an inspiring speech. *May your testimony bring pleasure from the gods. May your work be remembered for centuries. May you bring honor to our customs.*

Throughout the day messages came back and forth. Sometimes there was a long delay between word. But every time it was the same. The altar is assembled. The priests are worshiping. They call out the name of Baal. The people are watching with amazement. Surely they will all worship Baal soon.

The priests have become more fervent now. They are dancing. They are calling out louder and louder. They have just begun to cut themselves with their own swords. Their blood is flowing. Surely Baal will answer. But not to worry, nothing is happening for the prophet either. He mocks our priests and sits around waiting for something.

The day is almost ended. The people are tired. The priests are drenched in blood, sweat, and tears. Elijah has just begun to work, commanding that his servants use 12 stones to make an altar that pays homage to the 12 tribes of Israel. Such a simple man. Now they are digging a trench around the altar. Ha, what a waste of time. Next they are climbing up and down the mountain with buckets of water from the Dead Sea and drenching their sacrifice. *Don't worry my queen, he just looks crazier than ever.*

Ummmm queen, I have some bad news. He made such a simple prayer. We chuckled when we heard it. Elijah said: "God of Abraham, Isaac and Jacob I am your servant. Let it be known today that I am your servant and that we are your people." His mouth barely uttered an "AMEN" before a ball of fire was hurled from the sky. It consumed everything. And ummmm the people started shouting: "God, He is the God."

The messenger must be shaking in his boots. He is presenting upsetting information to an off-with-your-head queen. And she is capable of issuing such an order. The guards stand around him armed and capable of murder. He grits his teeth and steadies his shaking knees. He wonders if today is the end of the road for him. And in a stroke of pure luck she locks eyes with the messenger. She bellows: *May it be known today—if*

Elijah is not dead by the end of tonight, you may kill me. The messenger gulps hardly believing he was truly spared. He stands frozen until another bellow follows. Queen Jezebel says: *Don't waste a minute. Find him!* The messenger turns on his heels and makes his way back down the road to deliver the message.

Chapter 9:

Scarring

When the temperature begins to drop outside the tree stops providing nutrients to the leaf. This process is called scarring. It is the process that causes the leaf to turn colors. The once green leaf now turns orange, yellow, or red. It is the leaf's last *Horrah!* It's the brilliant exit one step before death.

Autumn is a season for survival. It is a time for mistakes and problems. In the fall it is time to take full responsibility for what has happened in the other seasons both the good and the bad. This time is an opportunity to learn from the previous seasons and prepare for the long winter by handling what you can. Don't get stuck in the cold without a coat.

Fall is a time for transitions. The developmental stage of fall is middle adulthood, 40 to 60 years old. Whether it is the disillusionment of our relationships, the limits of our physical bodies, or the many consequences of our choices, this stage has real emotional consequences. It often leaves us with the feeling of disappointment. Life's struggles begin to pile up and come together. We are left with two choices—embrace to accept or numb to avoid.

So far, Jezebel's efforts to eradicate worship of the Hebrew God were in vain. She has tried everything but could not vanquish the prophet Elijah. Similar to my efforts to avoid loss and ignore the deterioration of our church, fall can hard. It can also be beautiful Te physical season of fall straddles summer and winter. Change is in the air. As the leaves turn from rich green to bright orange the air turns from sweltering hot to a crisp cool. It is on those Indian summer days when the sun is warm and a sweater isn't necessary that it easy to forget that a freeze is coming.

When I was a little girl my mother would press flowers. We would find perfect purple violets and press them between wax paper preserving them for a time when the flowers would be covered by snow. We would also press leaves. We would search through the freshly fallen leaves under our tree for the most brilliant yellow or orange ones. Then we would press them. These leaves were in their third phase of the life cycle. They had been cut off from the tree and ushered into death and yet we celebrated them for their life.

Just as the process of maturation called scarring happens to a leaf, by the time we reach middle adulthood people have scars too. This season can be an opportunity to look at our scars. Disappointment, disillusionment, and disenchantment are exquisitely intimate emotions. Sometimes the dissolving of a dream is so painful that middle-aged adults quit dreaming. We must honor the wounds. Just as I used to make a collage of red, yellow, and orange leaves in the fall, do an accounting of your scars and honor them by looking at them. The scars left behind by life may be the reminders of wounds but they are also the celebrations of a life well lived.

Fall is a season of acceptance. It is time that offers an opportunity to evaluate mistakes and problems. Although the colors may be brilliant, they signal a change that is coming.

Activity C: The Season of Fall
Fall DISILLUSIONMENT – DISAPPOINTMENT – DESPONDENCY
Use the tree to create what Fall looks like in your life.
- What experience marked this time in your life?
- Use color, images, and words to describe what you felt during this season.
- Identify the experience, time, date, or circumstance of the season.

Reflect:

... then I will send rain on your land in its season, both autumn and spring rains, so that you may gather in your grain, new wine and olive oil. I will provide grass in the fields for your cattle, and you will eat and be satisfied.
– Deuteronomy 11:14-15

Process:

Take a look at your tree. What do you feel when it is Fall in your story?

Pray:

Dear Lord,

The season of Fall is a time of disillusionment. The brilliant colors of autumn are beautiful and yet indicate change. Please grant me strength as I transition between summer and winter. Amen

Winter: Death

Life asked death, why do people love me, but hate you? Death responded, because you are a beautiful lie and I'm a painful truth.
– author unknown

For you have delivered me from death
and my feet from stumbling,
that I may walk before God
in the light of life.
– Psalm 56:13

The fear of the LORD is a fountain of life,
turning a person from the snares of death.
– Proverbs 14:27

Chapter 10:

Dark and Cold

Night comes early in December in Wisconsin. It can be dark as early as 4 p.m. When I left the house at 7 p.m. the darkness was thick and it felt like midnight. I had just listened to a client share the terrifically tragic story that was called his life. The narrative was heavy like bricks and I could feel the weight resting on my shoulders. I felt like I was pushing through the darkness and in an instant my body was lurching, falling, clinging. I had slipped on black ice and fallen to the ground. There on the cold, hard ground I felt surprised and helpless. I remember grabbing for the handle of my car door and trying to figure out how to get up. I climbed into the seat of my little SUV, turned the key and slowly backed out of the drive way. Once on the road my tears began to fall. I cried, wailed, sobbed until I arrived home.

I reached the door of our house. The dark night was met with bright streams of light both from the lit house and the faces of my teenagers who were happy to see me. Then, as they surveyed their mother, their faces grew solemn and dark. Both teens scrambled to help asking if I needed to go to the emergency room. I shook my head no. My daughter said: *Come, sit down.*

I remember saying: *I don't think I will get back up.* So instead I went upstairs, shed my clothes, and got into bed. The tears had not stopped flowing. I lay there sore, worn out, sobbing.

It wasn't too long before my husband got home and promptly took over. His commanding voice said: *You will not be going to the training tomorrow. You will stay in bed, go to the chiropractor, and rest.*

This time my broom tree came as convalescence. The next morning I did go to the doctor. I had been struggling with a mysterious pain in my left arm for months. The doctor suggested that my ailment may have an emotional connection. She recommended a book that listed physical ailments, highlighting the emotional connections to parts of the human body. I got home from my appointment, wrapped up in a blanket, and opened the book: *You Can Heal Your Life* by Louise Hay. I skimmed through to read about the significance of pain in the left arm. Two words: *letting go*. I shut the book, turned on a Hallmark Christmas movie, and slept for six hours.

The next day I was re-energized and not so sore. I took the dog for a walk and carefully stepped avoiding the ice patches. It was outside, surrounded by frozen ground, leafless trees and death I cried out to God: *I'm not OK. I don't know what to do. I can't keep living this way.*

I don't hear an audible voice when God speaks. Rather he communicates with my spirit. It is imperative for me to stop talking and start listening. Although it is not a word out loud, it is an undeniable sense. God brings memories to mind. He reminds me of Scripture verses I have memorized. When I was out a walk in the desolate white abyss of winter, God asked: *Andrea, what did I last tell you to do?*

I finished my walk and after taking off my winter layers, I connected with the journal where I had scribbled notes from my October Cuba experience. In the 20 pages of notes written on our plane ride home I found the answer. While in Cuba I had the distinct sense that I was missing something at home. I felt God ask: *Why do you have to go so far away to teach The Elijah Project when there are people in your home town who could benefit from it?*

Reading my own notes left a gnawing feeling in my insides. I had a sense that in order to teach classes regularly, I would need to make some other changes to my schedule. Of course I had many reasons not to do that. I felt like we didn't have enough money for me to cut back at work. I believed we didn't have the physical space to accommodate my classes. And I knew I didn't have the emotional space in my heart to take this step apart from God.

As God conversations often go with me, it was a flicker. The words were crisp and vivid in the moment. I had a deep understanding of what God had said and just as quickly as the meaning came, real life took over. In a moment, the clarity of the intimate communion was gone. Dishes, laundry, driving kids to activities, and paperwork for my job took over; life was back in full swing.

Chapter 11:

When the Castle is All You Know

Do it again! He bellows. She kneels before the formidable statue and prays. She repeats the words she had been taught. The men in robes come toward her with a lifeless animal. It is a duck. The small slit in its neck allows blood to slowly seep out. *Catch the blood.* She looks away attempting to squeeze the blood out without looking. *JEZEBEL!*

Yes, Father! I know Father! I'm trying, she stammers.

We will stay here as long as it takes.

She feels the lump in her stomach get tighter. She knows that he will make her stay here until she meets his expectation.

From the tips of her toes to the top of her head she tightens every muscle in her body. She is not going to repeat the instruction again. She squares her shoulder, looks the duck in its eyes, tears up and squeezes. The feathers are soft as the limp flesh has its blood pressed out. Finally the shallow gold bowl is filled and the next part of the ritual can begin.

Good job, Jez! That's my girl.

The priests gather round wiping her hands as she feels a swell of fierce pride.

It will be easier every time, kid!

Somehow she believes he is right.

Sometime Later

She stands up with fire in her eyes approaching her servant. Even though she is shorter than the man dressed in armor, carrying a sword she is undaunted by his stature. Her husband, Ahab, stands close by. Having witnessed this scene before, he made certain that someone else carried the message. He simply states: *There is more to tell you my pet.*

Jezebel takes her boney finger and wags it in the guard's face. *Why you better have good news unlike the last guy.* She motions to a large blood stained patch on her stone floor. A young maiden looks up with fear in her eyes as she scrubs using horse hair bristles.

Ma'am. The guard stands a little straighter and subtly touches his sword. The guard doesn't say another word. King Ahab simply says: *They are gone.* Queen Jezebel steps back, startled. Ahab continues: *They dragged them down the mount...* As if dazed, she leaps back into the guard's space as her hands clasp around his neck. He gasps for air as she looks square into the eyes of her husband. The guard whimpers. She wants to crush his larynx—somehow making his words go away will silence her husband. She releases the pressure from around the guard's neck as if he is the one sharing the story.

He dragged them where? She is torn between a little more blood making her feel better and getting the rest of the story.

Ahab looks away. *Tell her.*

The always faithful, strapping palace soldier squeaks out his final words: *He killed them in the Kishon Valley.*

With one gesture she motions for her personal guard to kill him and squawks out a new message intended for the crazy prophet: *May the gods deal with me, be it ever so severely, if by this time tomorrow I do not make your life like that of one of them.*

Ahab, the guy in charge, stands stunned, silenced, and a little scared. A brutal man himself, his evil is often put to shame by the tyrannical acts of his wife. He wonders for a moment, *how had she become like this?* But then he reclines next to her and continues to fill his famished belly.

Jezebel cannot eat. The stone walls of her chambers close in around her. *Is this the end? Will this prophet of God be her demise?* Her insecurity is railing. In her mind the ancient words of her father, once a blessing, now a curse—*Make us proud. Be the leader we know you can be.*

A brilliant miracle had just occurred. Fire descended from heaven and connected with the prophet Elijah's altar like a kiss. The fire had swallowed up the sacrifice, the wood, the stones, and all the water that filled the trough around the altar. Word traveled fast, as if on the wings of a bird. Jezebel's priests were embarrassed and her power was threatened.

Jezebel has known winter before. She has lived winter many times over again. Growing up in a polytheistic culture desensitized her to sexual and physical violence. From the time of being a little girl, her scars hardened so that she has a thick skin. Jezebel is a perfect example of the victim becoming the abuser. She is a hurt person who hurts people. She is older, wiser, and more numb than ever now. As an adult, Jezebel's winter is marked by scorn for the prophet Elijah. Her face turns dark. Both sad and enraged, she vows that her story will not end here.

Chapter 12:

Brittle

The color is gone. The last bit of nourishment has reached the leaf and now it is becoming brittle and brown. The stem once strong and virile clinging to the leaf slowly becomes more and more dry. As the leaf travels towards starvation the onlookers enjoy brilliant colors. The red, orange, and yellow are signs that the leaf is no longer connected to its life source. By winter the nutrients once provided by the tree are a faint memory and the leaf is brown and lifeless. This is a visual picture of what happens with compound trauma. When one devastating thing happens after another, our emotional reserves run dry and we become less resilient, cold, and emotionally numb.

One can only imagine the nightmares that haunted Jezebel. While her trauma began in childhood, it is reinforced during adulthood through her own brutal behavior. She coped by enclosing herself inside a cocoon of hate and rage. The covering shielded her from intimacy and joy. The work it would take to break out of that cocoon must have seemed daunting. Her cruel life was so customary that a life outside of it probably seemed impossible. This downward spiral would ultimately seal her fate and reinforce her behavior even deeper.

Do you relate to Jezebel? Do you feel like you lack the momentum to change the downward spiral? When winter seems endless, it might be something else. In C.S. Lewis' *The Chronicles of Narnia* the White Witch traps the land in a spell. Narnia's woodland creatures described it as *always winter and never spring*. The aftermath of trauma can feel like that. Trauma is the suffering or pain that results from a deeply distressing or disturbing experience. Our bodies hold onto negative experiences and cope with them through stomach aches, racing thoughts, and a rapid heart rate.

God designed our brain to be resilient. Science says that the thalamic pathways or our reptilian brain are the place where lower order connections are made with the amygdala. This instinctual part of the brain does not analyze the circumstances to make a plan instead it reacts through fight, flight, or freeze. During times of stress, the brain going offline and transitioning into these autonomic responses allows it to survive. I wonder if these survival instincts are part of the Fall? I imagine there is no need for them during perfected life in the Garden. God said to Adam: ...***through painful toil you will eat all the days of your life. It will produce thorns and thistles for you...*** – Genesis 3:18. I think fight, flight, and freeze constitute as the thorns and thistles in our brains. When memories around a traumatic event are triggered the brain responds instinctively. When faced with a stressful situation a person may pick a fight becoming combative or run away or avoid the feeling all together. I freeze! My body becomes stuck and my thoughts loop in such a way that I feel helpless. From the outside I appear to be a 46-year-old professional woman but inside I feel overwhelmed, afraid, and uncertain how to defend myself.

I've worked in the mental health field for 25 years. When I first began my career as a therapist I worked at a residential program for girls. At that time most of my caseload experienced some kind of sexual trauma. There were a variety of diagnoses handed out in the late '90s but one of the most common for teenagers was bi-polar disorder. I was often frustrated with this diagnosis because although the symptoms fit the presenting behaviors of my clients, the diagnosis was accompanied by a strong medication protocol and a sort of life-sentence that this disease is now *who I am*. It felt very damning to label a 13-year-old that way. After hearing the stories of my clients I remember thinking: *I would act manic too* if that had happened to me. And when the children would come to therapy and report that their parents had not attended their weekend visitations, I would think: *I would feel deeply sad and hopeless too.*

In the past 10 to 15 years an incredible amount of research has emerged to explain the human body's response to trauma. In fact, the behaviors connected to trauma triggers can look a lot like a manic episode. Research also indicates that our brains form new nuero pathways to cope with abuse and this looks like what we knew of manic-depressive disorder. What this really indicates is that many of the women, who were too often put in sanitariums in the '30s and '40s and given shock therapy, were probably suffering from trauma. Humanity struggles when our loss is too great and cannot be balanced with our resilience; we are left in an emotionally fractured state. It is called a break down. We all experience the schism between control and losing it and sometimes it leads to a full emotional shut down. During these times medication is vitally important to keep us alive and help us function again. There is no shame in it. I heard Sheila Walsh share her testimony about mental illness and she frankly stated: *Don't stop taking your little blue pill.*

We can also learn to understand our triggers, observe our internal and external reactions, and develop coping skills that help us own our trauma story and live beyond it rather than just survive in it.

No one likes to feel out of control. One way to resume control is to detach. When we are hurt we often build walls to protect ourselves. To cope we compartmentalize our emotions and cut ourselves off from certain feelings. The fight, flight, and freeze responses are widely shared. In fact these are posted in our area elementary schools where I work. Jennifer Lefebre, PsyD, has expanded the basic responses to trauma to include *fool around, fidget, and faint.* Her work is so valuable. Sometimes our responses don't fit into just three categories. She explains that to fool around and fidget is to respond playfully and use humor to self-sooth. This gives us a whole new perspective on the class clown. And fainting is when a person goes into the freeze mode and then just lies down or collapses emotionally or physically. I love this expansion on the work because I think it more fully describes my reaction to stress.

I shared earlier that I respond to stress by freezing. One time, I was invited to teach a group of church leaders a mental health laity curriculum. It was the beginning of my foray back into public speaking after a ten year hiatus as a stay-at-home mother. I was so excited to share the groundbreaking curriculum that I had been a part of creating with a multidisciplinary team assembled by the Substance Abuse and Mental Health Services Administration. I arrived at the church early. The care minister who had invited me and I handed out the substantial information packets. I taught the six hour class to over 40 professional ministers. Although most people are surprised by this, it takes a great deal of inner strength for me to stand at the podium and teach. I have a lot of introvert traits. The suit I was wearing masked a deeply insecure mother of three.

The question and answer part was the most difficult. My inner critic was screaming: *You should go home and make oatmeal raisin cookies. You don't know what you are talking about. You have been out of the work world too long. You're ruining your three-year-old daughter by returning to work too early.* It was awful. It took every ounce of energy I had to stay standing upright. I couldn't get out of the room fast enough. I closed in prayer, cleaned up my supplies, and drove home. I recall bustling through the door of our home, running upstairs, dropping my bag, and kicking off my shoes; I couldn't crawl under the covers fast enough. It was like I fell asleep before I hit the pillow. I slept for two hours. When I woke up I was OK. My heart had stopped racing and my thinking brain had returned. My husband looked at me with love and dread on his face: *Are you OK? What happened?*

I think he expected me to share that I tripped on the way to the stage or blanked out and couldn't speak. I remember looking at him with a penetrating honesty and saying: *I don't know.* And that was the truth. I didn't know because the stress of speaking had caused my brain to go off line. I had survived just long enough to retreat inside myself and go to sleep. Now I understand better; I had emotionally fainted.

Of course in the ancient world people didn't have words to describe the way the brain worked. There was no fancy diagnosis for Jezebel. Instead she wore beautiful clothes, royal jewels, and a crown to mask her unresolved pain and abuse. For Jezebel it is likely that her abuse occurred in the castle or at the temple. When our home or family does not protect us, it adds another level to the trauma, forcing us to protect ourselves. One of the best forms of self-protection is to build a wall. We do it all the time. We build walls around the most vulnerable parts of our hearts, souls, and minds. Jezebel lived within a unique set of circumstances. As a queen she held power and influence that most of us do not possess. She could extravagantly adorn herself in an attempt to compensate for her deep emotional wounds. She engaged hired help to join her in life, people who were paid to stay by her side. She had not garnered loyalty from deep intimate friendship and love. Instead she had paid staff.

The Bible records the end of Jezebel's life like this:

> ***Then Jehu went to Jezreel. When Jezebel heard about it, she put on eye makeup, arranged her hair and looked out of a window. As Jehu entered the gate, she asked, "Have you come in peace, you Zimri, you murderer of your master?"***
>
> ***He looked up at the window and called out, "Who is on my side? Who?" Two or three eunuchs looked down at him. "Throw her down!" Jehu said. So they threw her down, and some of her blood spattered the wall and the horses as they trampled her underfoot.***
> *– 2 Kings 9:30-32*

In the end Jezebel's unresolved life ends up as a fractured heap on the ground. She greeted the new ruler with a sense of hope that he was going to join her in her ways. But instead Jehu asked if the kingdom supported him. Jezebel's hired help probably exhausted by years of terrible treatment jumped at the chance to push her out the window—a dismal end to a devastating life. Jezebel's life had many times of winter but I think this was the worst. Her makeup and perfectly coiffed hair could not cover her life of revenge.

Jezebel built walls around her heart just like the walls of her kingdom. She turned her anger outward. While she may have gained physical ground for the Northern Kingdom she lived emotionally detached from other people. Her emotional detachment made her violent life easier. I am not like Jezebel. When I feel the isolation, the dark and cold of winter, it translates into sadness. When my dreams die or life stages end I feel like the brittle leaf literally crunching under someone's foot or being buried by inches of white snow. I feel heavy, lonely, and trapped. As winter comes and goes throughout life, we are left with opportunities to develop healthy coping skills through art, music, and recreation. Some coping strategies for winter include prayer, relaxation, journaling, sharing, and breathing. These activities can foster joy and connection. The choice to close off, stiffen our bodies, and isolate can freeze off areas of our hearts and minds, reducing self-expression and leaving us alone.

Above the ground winter looks desolate, as though everything is dead. Below the ground something good is happening. Seeds are germinating and sending out roots. Like the seeds we can move toward spring, even as we endure the winter. In *The Four Seasons of Transformation* Jim Rohn writes: *winter is a season of reflection, hibernation, and planning.* Developing healthy ways of coping during warmer seasons can provide the reserve we need to traverse the winters. If winter has taken its toll, you may feel dry and brittle on the outside. Look to cultivate a small seed of joy within yourself. Remember a happy memory and journal about it. Pick up a once-loved hobby and start doing it. Re-read your favorite book or watch your favorite movie. Plant and nurture some seeds of hope.

Activity D: The Season of Winter
Winter DEATH – ENDINGS – CLOSURE
Use the tree to create what Winter looks like in your life.
- What experience marked this time in your life?
- Use color, images, and words to describe what you felt during this season.
- Identify the experience, time, date, or circumstance of the season.

Reflect:

The L*ORD *smelled the pleasing aroma and said in his heart: "Never again will I curse the ground because of human, even though every inclination of the human heart is evil from childhood. And never again will I destroy all living creatures, as I have done."

"As long as the earth endures, seedtime and harvest, cold and heat, summer and winter, day and night will never cease."
– Genesis 8:21-22

Process:

Take a look at your tree. What do you feel when it is Winter in your story?

Pray:

Dear God,

I struggle with winter. I feel dark, lonely, and disconnected. Please embrace me, draw me close as I walk through winter. Amen

---

[1] *If the winter chapter resonated with you and you question if your winter has lasted longer than what is healthy, consider reaching out for help. Don't try to navigate winter alone.* **Call this number now for 24 hour help: 1-800-273-8255.** This is the national suicide prevention line with counselors who can help.

Sacred Seasons

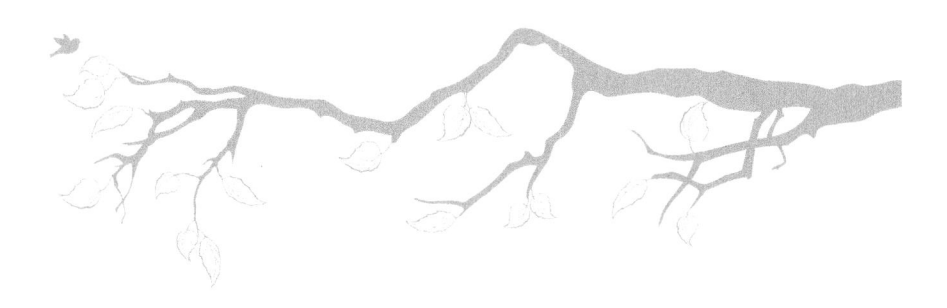

You can't go back and change the beginning, but you can start where you are and change the ending.
– C.S. Lewis

His divine power has given us everything we need for a godly life through our knowledge of him who called us by his own glory and goodness.
– 2 Peter 1:3

Say to those with fearful hearts,
"Be strong, do not fear;
your God will come,
he will come with vengeance,
with divine retribution
he will come to save you."
– Isaiah 35:4

Chapter 13:

The Season You Find Yourself In

Elijah has a sacred moment at the broom tree. He experiences a holy meeting and is ministered to by an angel. After receiving nourishment and rest he embarks on a 40-day journey to Mount Horeb. This is the same mountain where God met Moses and delivered the Ten Commandments. Elijah climbed the mountainous terrain and once he got to the top he crawled into a cave. Suddenly there was a great earthquake but God was not in the earthquake. Then there was a great wind but God was not in the wind. Then there was a fire but God was not in the fire. He was not in any of the natural disasters. God spoke in a gentle whisper. From within the cave Elijah heard the voice of God inquire: *Elijah, what are you doing here?*

Elijah responded to God's inquiry with a litany of justifications, saying, *I've been zealous for you God and now you have left me all alone.* You can almost hear the whine in his rambling.

God asks Elijah two more times why he is there and two more times Elijah responds defensively, questioning God's ways and complaining about the outcomes. Perhaps, when Elijah set off running he ended up in the opposite direction further from what God planned not closer. This exchange suggests to me that possibly Elijah didn't go where God had directed when he left the broom tree. This summation is affirmed when God says: *Go back from where you came and appoint Jehu as King and Elisha as your mentee.*

There is a beautiful candor in this exchange between God and Elijah. God inquires over and over again: *What are you doing here?* Elijah in turn defends himself by rehearsing all the reasons he is there. But in the end, God says: *This isn't where I want you to be* and gives him directions to go back the way he came. I believe this little bit of Scripture is all about acceptance. God isn't arguing with Elijah about where he is. He isn't shaming Elijah for not following. He is asking Elijah to admit where he is.

I often struggle to accept the places I find myself when I run off course. When I become emotionally overwhelmed one of my coping mechanisms is to gossip. I think it will feel better to exploit others' weaknesses with my words but I always end up feeling worse than I did before. When I gain weight, I cope by buying new clothes. This doesn't work well for me because I will refuse to buy the next size up so I just end up having another outfit that doesn't fit right. It would have been more productive to go for a power walk rather than spend money. When I really want to avoid God I binge on a television show, retreating to the safety of my bedroom where I keep a pile of great resources next to my bed: a Bible, a journal, a new pen (I love fun pens), and the current book I'm reading. Sometimes I go to the effort of laying everything next to me on the bed, but then I turn on the television and become absorbed with someone else's life and the books stay closed, pen unused.

I think Christians experience a particularly difficult time with acceptance because there is an inherent belief that God isn't happy when He sees us. In other words, God is somehow disappointed when He finds us in the mess of a mistake or in the pain of brokenness. This is just not true. Throughout Jesus' parables He depicts the power of finding the thing that is lost—the lost sheep, the lost coin, and the lost son. I believe that evangelical Christians struggle with acceptance the most because we allow ourselves only a fleeting moment in being found. In those found moments we hear *I love you too much to leave you here*—something that I do not believe God really says. Yes, God has an abundant life for us, but He isn't in a hurry to get us there. Jesus, fully God, modeled the journey during His 33 years of life as man. He walked, He ate, He communed and struggled through real life with His disciples. It is simply untrue that He expected whirlwind transformation. What He did expect was that the Light only He could bring would produce change.

The *loving us too much to leave us there* idea produces a sense that we must confess and get over the messy parts of our story. I believe Jesus modeled walking through the storm. The power of acceptance means that we look at ourselves, our life as it truly is, our strengths and weaknesses, our successes and failures as they are, and embrace all of them. To embrace difficulty takes a great deal of courage. It means we drop the facade and feel all the feelings that accompany this phase of life. A simplistic example in my life means reading the numbers on the scale and writing these down accurately; acknowledging my real weight, not fudging it to be the weight I want it to be. Looking at the number, saying it out loud, and keeping track of it in my calorie counter empowers me to produce true change. As we accept the truth that is, it also allows the people around us to feel what they feel. It takes away the crazy-making feeling because we now weep with those who weep and laugh when others are laughing.

I believe we can only accept reality if we believe that God can accept us in this reality. The Bible says that while we were still sinners God died for us. The gift of Jesus was given for us, not despite us. Jesus died for us right in the middle of our story. If God could make a way for us knowing we had failed, would fail, and will fail, falling short of His plan, then we possess holy permission to accept the place we find ourselves. If I can accept that God truly loves me just as I am, then I can be the person I was created to be. This process allows God to be God and me to be me.

Bill W., the founder of Alcoholics Anonymous, developed the most effective program for dealing with alcoholism because he first accepted his struggle with alcohol and then he spent hours trying to help others quit drinking. Below is a great excerpt from the *Big Book of AA* that summarizes what we are learning.

Acceptance Was The Answer

Excerpt from Alcoholics Anonymous, the *Big Book*, pg 417

And acceptance is the answer to all of my problems today. When I am disturbed, it is because I find some person, place, thing or situation—some fact of my life—unacceptable to me, and I can find no serenity until I accept that person, place, thing, or situation as being exactly the way it is supposed to be at this moment. Nothing, absolutely nothing, happens in God's world by mistake. Until I could accept my alcoholism, I could not stay sober; unless I accept life completely on life's terms, I cannot be happy. I need to concentrate not so much on what needs to be changed in the world as on what needs to be changed in me and in my attitudes.

As Christians it can be difficult to accept life as it is because we know this is not all there is. Jesus said: *There will be suffering in this world but take heart, I have overcome the world.*

There is a tenuous balance between accepting earthly life as it is while looking forward to eternity in heaven. The most difficult part of life is accepting hardship as a way to peace (*The Serenity Prayer*). The process of accepting life as it truly is right now, taking time to understand the way I respond to my struggles, and living the best I can within my pain requires ownership of the true.

The second section of this book is called *Sacred Seasons*. These chapters tie the spiritual, emotional, and physical all together using creative activities. The activities offer opportunities to pause and celebrate accomplishments and provide space to grieve losses. They offer an invitation to identify places and spaces where you may be stuck. Often difficult memories cloud our ability to truly rejoice in the good. The practical part of this book is like putting on your own oxygen mask on an airplane. We must do our own work first so that we can wholly connect with our family and friends, and if we want to truly help others.

Activity E: What season are you in?
Use the tree to depict the season you are in right now.

Spring – A time of hope and promise for the future, often marked by learning and new opportunities.

Summer – A time of life filled with abundance, growing, and development, often marked by enjoying the rewards of hard work, celebration, and fulfillment.

Fall – A time of life when we experience disappointment and disillusionment, a time often marked by making mistakes and the discouragement of suffering consequences.

Winter – A season of hibernation, reflection, and planning, often marked by grief or loss.

What words describe the current state of your journey?

Reflect:
And God said, "Let there be lights in the vault of the sky to separate the day from the night, and let them serve as signs to mark sacred times, and days and years, and let them be lights in the vault of the sky to give light on earth." And it was so. God made two great lights—the greater light to govern the day and the lesser lights to govern the night. He also made the stars. God set them in the vault of the sky to give light on the earth, to govern the day and the night, and to separate light from darkness. And God saw that it was good. And there was evening, and there was morning.
– Genesis 1:14-19

Process:
Take a look at your tree. What do you notice about how you are feeling: your successes and your stresses?

Does anything surprise you in what you see?

Pray:
Dear God,
Please enter into my story. May I feel your presence, comfort, and peace as I accept the place where I find myself. Amen

Chapter 14:

Seasons of Emotion

Learning to express my feelings has been a process. When I was in high school I don't really remember talking about how I felt. In college as I began to take social work classes I was challenged to express myself in context of my emotions. I don't have an accurate recollection of how I expressed myself but I think I mostly verbally vomited to whoever would listen. I was not responsible with my own emotions and I confused sharing my feelings with anyone who would listen to intimacy in relationship.

During the early years of our marriage I had very poor patterns for feeling expression. I would stuff my emotions and then misappropriate my frustration to places I felt were more socially appropriate. I used my emotions to manipulate situations and often said to myself: *You make me so mad, or because you did this, I feel this.* It has taken years and years of hard work for me to own my emotions within situations and then decipher when it is appropriate or safe to share those feelings.

Imagine a little ball of energy. What does it look like? What does it feel like? What does it produce? Each person is made up of many different kinds of energy. The divine spark from birth brings life, physical growth, emotional awareness, spiritual conscience, and relational connection. Those balls of energy rotate, move, and collide, generally pressing a person forward in her life cycle. Now take these imaginary balls of energy and give them color—red, blue, green, and yellow. I like to think of the red ball as anger or passion; the blue ball as sadness or grief; the green one as fear or anxiety; and the yellow one as joy and happiness. Just like the molecules that make up the human body (giving it form and function) the emotional energy in our bodies can be organized or unorganized. Many times life experiences can twist our emotions and leave us feeling chaotic or out of control.

There is a flow in a person's spirit that naturally progresses through the emotions. Feelings help to motivate, support, validate, and comfort. Breaking down emotions into four main categories can help to organize the otherwise swirling effect of our feelings. The bundle of disorganized emotional energy can be overwhelming and cloud clear thinking.

Spring is a time where the earth receives more sun and warmth. The emotions related to spring include: expectancy, happiness, hope, and peace. Summer is the time when days are longer, the sun is brighter, and the emotions have even more energy: joy, excitement, elation, passion. Fall often ushers in a sense of change, which can feel out of control and bring a sense of fear. Fear is a powerful emotion that can signal the body that there is danger up ahead. It can trap people, persuading us to stay stagnant, frozen, and stuck. Some of the fear emotions are scared, frightened, apprehensive, concerned, nervous, and anxious. Finally, winter is a time for hibernation, quiet, reflection, and seclusion. The emotions of this season include: blue, sadness, depression, and exhaustion.

Anger is a secondary emotion and it can be attached to each of the above groups of emotion. Anger is a category of emotion associated with the sense of being violated or wronged. The other side of anger can be sadness. We may feel mad-sad when a personal violation leads to the death of something. The other side of anger can be passion: when injustice is ignited. Passion is the happy or hopeful side of anger. Anger can also be the other side of fear: when the loss of innocence collides with the desire to keep oneself safe. It is easy to recognize anger and frustration in children. When a child's will is violated anger bubbles up in the form of fighting, yelling, and kicking. Sometimes when it is really overwhelming a caregiver needs to pick up the child, separate him from the situation, and hold him. This is because those imaginary balls of energy have become so disregulated that the child cannot bring them back into order fast enough to avoid causing damage to himself or others.

Adults do this too. Have you ever been in a meeting where someone becomes frustrated and slams her hands on the table, her face turns red, and then she says everything she is thinking, appropriate to the situation or not? The same thing has happened for the adult. Something about the discussion activated her emotions and she becomes so disregulated that she cannot hold her feelings in anymore. Generally everything spills out in this moment, often much more than what the original offense was. I imagine that a person came to your mind immediately. We all have poorly regulated adults in our lives. It might be Uncle Earl who always gets drunk at Thanksgiving and ends the evening in a fight. In order to avoid becoming old Uncle Earl we must become aware of our own emotional spheres. By identifying our feelings, owning them, and becoming aware of our triggers, we can adopt habits that allow us to regulate our emotions even when we are activated.

I have the most difficulty sharing my anger in real time with real people. I have a bad habit of sharing my frustration to a secondary person, venting to someone outside the relationship, and not addressing the violation with the violator. I am working on shutting off the inappropriate vents and using a journal to process my feelings. While I have not achieved mastery of this, I now realize that when I vent outside the relationship I am leaking. If I am able to quit talking and start to journal, it feels better. Sometimes I find myself processing the frustration and the guilt of the inappropriate behavior together. I continue to struggle to gain the inner strength to harness the negative emotions, put words to them, and share them with the person who offended me. Although I am getting better, this is where my people pleasing most often creeps in and usurps the good habits I am trying to own.

The following activity will give you an opportunity to process your own unique emotional make up. As you pay attention to what each ball of emotional energy feels like inside of you, try to express it with words and colors so that the next time these emotions bubble up you can use your self-awareness to process in a healthy way.

Activity F: The Feeling Leaf

Use the leaves on the next page to make your own feelings list. Identify five unique words for each feeling category: Joy, Sadness, Fear, and Anger. Use words that fit your personality and the way you define your emotional world.

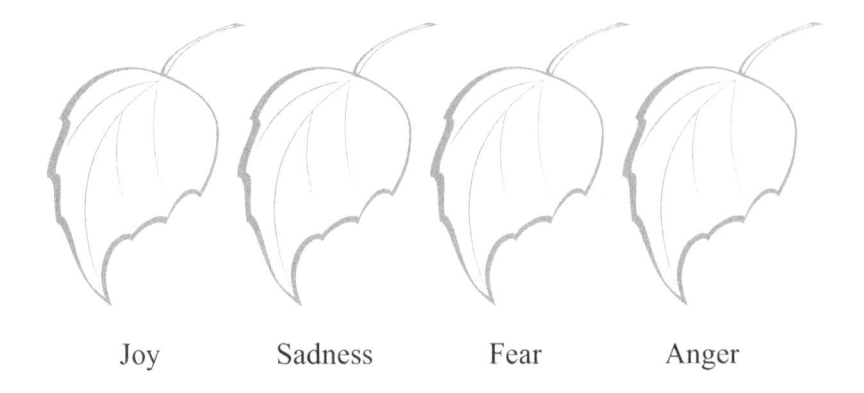

| Joy | Sadness | Fear | Anger |

Reflect:
God's word offers framework for our emotions. Below are some Scripture passages that provide spiritual context to our feelings.

Joy

But the fruit of the Spirit is love, joy, peace, forbearance, kindness, goodness, faithfulness, gentleness and self-control. Against such things there is no law.
– Galatians 5:22-23

Sadness

*The Spirit of the Sovereign L*ORD *is on me,*
  *because the L*ORD *has anointed me*
  to proclaim good news to the poor.
He has sent me to bind up the brokenhearted,
  to proclaim freedom for the captives
  and release from darkness for the prisoners,
*to proclaim the year of the L*ORD*'s favor*
  and the day of vengeance of our God,
to comfort all who mourn,
  and provide for those who grieve in Zion—
to bestow on them a crown of beauty
  instead of ashes,

the oil of joy
 instead of mourning,
and a garment of praise
 instead of a spirit of despair.
They will be called oaks of righteousness,
 a planting of the LORD
 for the display of his splendor.
– Isaiah 61:1-3

Fear

If you fear the LORD and serve and obey him and do not rebel against his commands, and if both you and the king who reigns over you follow the LORD your God—good!
– 1 Samuel 12:14

Anger

Therefore each of you must put off falsehood and speak truthfully to your neighbor, for we are all members of one body. "In your anger do not sin": Do not let the sun go down while you are still angry, and do not give the devil a foothold. Anyone who has been stealing must steal no longer, but must work, doing something useful with their own hands, that they may have something to share with those in need.
– Ephesians 4:25-28

Process:

How do your emotions affect your daily life?

Are your emotions good influences or harmful ones?

How do the Scriptures above challenge your perspective on these common feeling words?

How does your faith in God influence how you view your emotions?

Pray:
Dear Lord,
I struggle with _____. I appreciate that You created my emotions as a gift to help me live more fully. At times, I struggle to balance my emotions. Please govern over me so that I am able to hang on in the tension between the good and bad sides of my feelings, that I may experience freedom in my emotions. Amen

Chapter 15:

Seasons of the Spirit

We have identified what physical season we are in. We have looked at our emotions in context of the seasons. Now we will look more closely at Spiritual seasons. I find the idea of Spiritual seasons both life giving and frustrating. Identifying that there are seasons in my walk with God helps me feel less crazy and reduces the feeling that I am doing something wrong because I cannot hear Him. At the same time it is frustrating because I want God to take the difficult season away. I am in company with King Solomon when he said:

> ***For everything there is a season,***
> ***a time for every activity under heaven.***
> *– Ecclesiastes 3:1 NLT*

In *Ecclesiastes* Solomon laments that God has ordained the things that happen in our lives and that He has given us seasons. Courtnaye Richard has identified five Spiritual seasons that we can add to our discussion of seasons.

1. First is the ***Dry Season*** is when God is quiet or you can't hear His voice or sense His presence as you once did.
2. Next is the ***Waiting Season*** which is marked by planning, pruning, and stripping away what's not needed for the next season in life.
3. There is the ***Grinding Season***, a busy time when there doesn't seem to be enough hours in the day. I often describe this time as having too many good, Godly things to do.
4. Then there is the ***Tests and Trials Season***, a time to press on even when you are weary in doing good.
5. Finally, the ***Spiritual Warfare Season*** is a time to recognize that the battle is with principalities and powers and things not of this world that cannot be fought alone.

I like the way that Courtnaye Richard organizes the Spiritual seasons. She has identified the difficult times in our spiritual walk well. I would like to add a season of celebration.

6. The ***Celebration Season*** is a time when we rejoice that God has protected and provided for us. It is a time when we recognize His hand and see His work in our lives.

Now let's visualize our leaf. It has changed color and texture and now it progresses through a spiritual phase. The leaves hung on to their branch all winter long (grinding season) until the new buds of spring poked up underneath. The new pushes at the old while the familiar clings on. Though the wind blows (spiritual warfare season) the leaves will not shake off. In my life it is difficult to wait for this process to happen, for the leaf to fall off. I want to shake and pull the leaves off before the new bud is ready to emerge. In *Isaiah 55:9* God says:

> ***As the heavens are higher than the earth,***
> ***so are my ways higher than your ways***
> ***and my thoughts than your thoughts.***

Although it may be human nature to push through one season to the next, God's timing is beyond what we can see or comprehend.

I have been a Christian for over 40 years and during that time I have walked through all of the Spiritual seasons multiple times. I have often felt the dry season (the Lord is quiet) or the grinding season (working hard to accomplish the most recent direction God gave me). The waiting season, which for me is often accompanied by terrific spiritual warfare, is most difficult. I really don't like to wait. I want to see the end from the beginning. I am good at planning and once I have laid out my meticulous plan, I want to see it happen. *Isaiah 40:31* says:

> ***but those who hope in the L***ORD
> ***will renew their strength.***

In the original language *hope* is translated wait. As a little girl I memorized *those who wait upon the Lord will renew their strength, they will mount up on wings as eagles, they will walk and not faint.* As a little girl I imagined the word wait to mean serving. I imagined Cinderella waiting on her step-sisters. I looked for ways to polish God's gigantic shoes. I served God as my task-master. Redefining waiting as hoping reframes the entire verse. Suddenly there is a promise at the end of the silence. There is an expectation of something more beyond the grind.

The Israelites went through seasons of their own. Most notably they had a season of slavery in Egypt and a season of deliverance. It was during the season of deliverance that Miriam sings. She says:

> ***I will sing to the LORD,***
> ***   for he is highly exalted.***
> ***Both horse and driver***
> ***   he has hurled into the sea.***
> *– Exodus 15:1*

Often Christians forget the step of celebration. It is often easier to list the difficult things that occur in life, renting our clothes in anguish rather than remember the times God has protected and provided for us. God is looking for complete connection with Him. He wants to celebrate when it is appropriate to celebrate. For the Israelites after the season of celebration came a season of wandering and finally a season of settling. Throughout each of their seasons, they consistently struggled with idol worship. But it wasn't until their season of settling that they first asked for a king. This was a very strategic request because it defied the very essence of the First Commandment.

> ***"I am the LORD your God, who brought you***
> ***out of Egypt, out of the land of slavery.***
> ***You shall have no other gods before me."***
> *– Exodus 20:2-3*

By putting a person in the role of leader, the Israelites supplanted the supremacy of God and broke His commandment—put God first. They were frustrated with the leadership of Samuel's sons and in their frustration they said they wanted to be like all the other nations of the world. They wanted a monarchy too. God warned the people but they stepped outside of God's plan and a new season was ushered in. The new rule brought with it a whole host of problems not the least of which includes the consequence of bad leaders like Ahab.

Today, as people of God, we continue to struggle to submit to His control. I mentioned Bill W. and the *Big Book* in Chapter 13. One of the core competencies of AA is to accept that you are powerless and need something beyond yourself. It doesn't seem to matter whether it was the Torah being read out in the wilderness, the *Old Testament* being read in many churches, or the 12 Steps being recited in an AA meeting. There is a universal understanding that we need something beyond ourselves in order to survive and thrive.

History can be a powerful mirror. Taking the time to reflect on our family lineage and personal patterns can help us circumvent some of the traps. When we do not heed what has come before, we are doomed to repeat it. I believe the most powerful force in the universe is self-sacrifice and the only innocent man to model true love and die for the depths of brokenness is Jesus Christ.

This activity provides a creative way to wrestle with the Spiritual seasons. It provides space for you to consider all the Spiritual seasons and when you have experienced them. Space is also provided for you to identify what Spiritual season you are in right now.

Activity G: My Spiritual Leaf
Identify experiences you have had in each of the Spiritual seasons:
- Dry season
- Waiting season
- Grinding season
- Tests and Trials season
- Spiritual Warfare season
- Celebration season

Below, create a leaf to represent each of the different Spiritual seasons, then identify which Spiritual season you are in today.

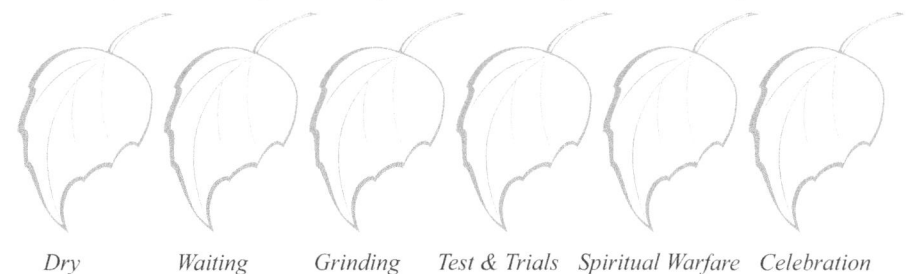

Dry   Waiting   Grinding   Test & Trials   Spiritual Warfare   Celebration

Reflect:
What does it mean for you to embrace God's words:

***There is a time for everything,
and a season for every activity under the heavens.***
– Ecclesiastes 3:1

***He made the moon to mark the seasons,
and the sun knows when to go down.***
– Psalm 104:19

Process:
How has looking at life through the framework of seasons given you greater perspective and hope for your future?

What is the most difficult Spiritual season for you to be in?

What are some strategies that help you work through difficult seasons rather than skip over them?

Pray:
Dear Lord,

I don't like the trying seasons. I get tired and long for the warmth of spring. Please draw close to me as I process through the season of _____ so that I don't skip over it and set a trap for myself in the future. I love you Jesus. Amen

Chapter 16:

Seasons of Grief

I will never forget how I felt the first time a close family member died. My Aunt Lucy was a four-foot-nothing white haired firecracker who always spoke her mind. I remember her rocking in the sitting room surrounded by a cloud of cigarette smoke while she crocheted. She made us everything you could think of from sweaters, to mittens, to afghans. She battled a long bout of cancer and I remember Grammy (her sister) telling us that Aunt Lucy had woken from her coma and said a few words. Grammy (my grandmother) had such hope. It was only a few days after her last words that Lucy passed. I was a child. I went to school the morning of her funeral and couldn't think. I remember just folding my arms on my desk and sobbing until it was time to be picked up. My Uncle George passed next but my level of emotion was not the same. Then, while I was away at seminary, my Great Aunt Lillian died, and that didn't hit me as hard either. The rest of my grandparents' siblings died when I was an adult, having lived good lives and it felt like it was time for them to go.

Modern psychology has accepted the body of work by Elisabeth Kübler-Ross MD and co-author David Kessler as the authority on the process of grief. In their famous book *On Grief and Grieving* they observed and described a linear journey. Their five steps—Denial, Anger, Bargaining, Depression, and Acceptance—are now accepted as canon for hospice workers around the world. Their research revealed that an individual facing a terminal diagnosis will experience all five stages of grief before reaching acceptance as he/she faces death.

Brochures based on Kübler-Ross' insights are given out by chaplains and hospital workers to both the infirmed and the family. The stages of grief help put into context the emotional journey of the person who is ill as she or he begins to walk through the loss. The five stages are a tool designed for the individual facing death. But what about the person facing an imminent loss? And what do you do, as one of the living, with all the emotions once the loss occurs?

There is much to do in the aftermath of a death: plan a funeral, finalize the estate, and return a mountain of casserole dishes. Often the loved ones left behind just try to survive during this time. This is normal and should be expected. There are many wonderful resources for loss related to death. My good friend Renee Wurzer has written a wonderful memoir called *Widowspeak: a Story of Grief and Joy* that illustrates the twisted path of grief after an unexpected death strikes.

Although the Kübler-Ross concepts are important to understand, this chapter is not designed for person who is dying, it is for the person left behind after the death. The bereaved experience the five stages of grief identified above but the process is less systematic. Much like a tangled ball of yarn, the emotions of the grieved become tangled up together. In my clinical experience I often hear people struggle with a combination of anger and sadness. The emotions can linger far beyond accepting the finality of the loss. When the one who is grieving begins to regain his or her energy (many times years after the death) and can finally look at the tangled ball of yarn, the process of untangling quickly leads to discovering the first knot. The knot is a place of stuckness, an emotional space where the griever must process in order to move to the next knot and untangle the next emotions trapped there. As you can imagine, this process can be long and painful. The human psyche would prefer to avoid the pain of unraveling the tangle and leave the knots intact.

Individuals experience the stages of grief after all sorts of losses not just the death of a person. Seasons bring birth and rebirth. In the natural order, to be reborn there must be an accompanying passing. The most elusive grief is the death of a dream. We often have hope that keeps us yearning, longing, and pressing forward to see the culmination of a dream for a child, for a marriage, or for a career. But when the dream does not come true the emotional aftermath has the same intensity as the feeling of losing a loved one. After a dream is lost a sort of winter sets in and the need to hibernate can lead to isolation and depression. It is important to recognize and value loss as a powerful force that can keep us feeling withered, lifeless, and stuck.

My paternal grandmother adored her grandchildren. She had always wanted nine children herself but due to pregnancy complications she was only able to have one child, my father. She exuded unconditional love for my father, my mother (her daughter-in-law), and all four of us kids (her grandchildren). She was the epitome of the cookies-and-milk grandmother. She always had candy in her home and when we slept over we watched the Lawrence Welk show after the Congregational Church bean supper. I have very fond memories of my grandmother. She died quite suddenly while I was living in Louisville, Kentucky. I will always remember where I was standing when we got the news. My mother was visiting because I was a new mother myself and my husband was on his first mission trip to Africa. My father called to tell us that my grandmother had been admitted to the hospital. The doctor was observing her and would give us a thorough report in the morning. My dad had returned home to get something to eat and rest. When he reached home the doctor called to report she was gone. When he called to tell us, I was standing in my apartment at the top of the stairs. A picture of the exterior panel of the bathroom door is engrained in my head to this day. There was no opportunity to say goodbye.

The death I remember the most is my Great Aunt Helen. I was living in Chippewa Falls, Wisconsin. And I again had a nine-month-old baby, our third child, daughter Jael. This time I was sitting in an Arby's after church when I received the call that my parents had found my aunt after a fall and that she had been hospitalized. I remember my mom saying: *You don't need to come yet, we don't know her prognosis yet.* I also remember looking across the booth at my husband and sharing the news. Aunt Helen was dear to him as well because we had all grown close when we lived together for two years in her home in Ipswich, Massachusetts. My husband and I also had a deal: *No regrets.* I'm not sure he said anything out loud but I can see his face in my mind when I remember that day—his gentle nod signaling what I should do.

By the time Jael and I flew to Boston and arrived at the hospital, Aunt Helen's speech was barely intelligible. I approached the bed and squeezed her hand. She said: *Andrea.* I was able to tell her everything I wanted to say. I told her I loved her and appreciated her. She didn't speak again after uttering my name.

I remember the eerie silence in the hospital room. This was the first time I ever heard the death rattle. Shortly after the rattle began my mother, father, brother, and I grabbed hands and prayed around Aunt Helen's bed. She took her last raspy breath while we prayed and then she was gone. We stood around her dead body. That was the first time I had ever watched someone die.

Aunt Helen was 96 years old when she passed away. She had an authentic faith and I have hope knowing we will meet again in heaven. This was a death I was able to do well. Acceptance came easier for me because I had no regrets.

When death comes quickly or unexpectedly there are often many regrets for the living. As an individual attempts to accept his or her loss, he/she may experience a sense of denial, intense anger, bargaining, and even a refusal to accept. Tangled with these responses is a sense of great sadness or depression. The process can take months and even years before full acceptance is reached. Compound grief is what happens when one loss piles on top of another loss. When a new loss occurs before the first loss is processed and accepted, it is as though grief is interrupted. Each new loss triggers the memories and feelings of the previous loss and it can feel overwhelming.

In my community we have had a rise in suicides among Caucasian men 55 to 65 years old. At first it seemed unusual. Why would men who were employed with families want to end their lives? But in accordance with the construct of compound grief it makes sense. By the time a man (in particular) with all the social and emotional responsibilities reaches 50 years old he has experienced a tremendous amount of loss. He may have known the loss of the dream of a happy marriage, a successful career, and his physical youth. No matter how fit you may be, age does a number on your body and requires more energy not less to keep it moving. Job loss, children leaving for college, and changes within romantic relationships accumulate. The emotions that follow can feel overwhelming and lead to the hopelessness. Once hopelessness gives way to despair, ending one's life can feel like the best answer.

I was watching an episode of *Cardboard Karaoke* with James Corden. He did a 30-minute segment with Paul McCartney. I didn't grow up listening to the Beatles; in fact I really didn't grow up hearing secular music at all, but I guess you had to grow up under a rock to not know who the Beatles are. As soon as James and Paul began to sing, I was surprised by how many Beatles' lyrics I actually knew. During the segment the two men sang as they took a drive down memory lane visiting some of the historic landmarks that are part of McCartney's music.

The story that struck me the most was about a dream Paul had after his mother passed away. He shared that his mother came to him and said: *Let it Be. It's gonna be all right, just let it be.*

This story caused me to look up the lyrics to *Let it Be*. The words are simple, yet profound:

> *When I find myself in times of trouble Mother Mary comes to me. Speaking words of wisdom, let it be. And in my hour of darkness she is standing right in front of me speaking words of wisdom, let it be. And when the broken hearted people living in the world agree there will be an answer, let it be. And when the night is cloudy there is still a light that shines on me, shine until tomorrow, let it be.*

Seeing Paul McCartney on screen, now much older than when he originally wrote *Let it Be* brought a new depth to the song. The words hung in the air around me. I had a moment of profound understanding as I thought of Paul's very prominent life and the depth of his losses: his mother, his music partner John Lennon, and his wife Linda McCartney, to name a few. No amount of money or fame has insulated Paul McCartney from grief.

Exploring loss is crucial for all of us because it effects how we live our lives. The visual picture of the dead oak leaf clinging to its branch illustrates the process of grief well. Even though the branch is feeding a new bud and that new life is growing, the old hangs on. It is almost like each bit of acceptance of a loss pushes the leaf from its stem. The process must repeat itself over and over before the new bud has enough inertia to push that dead leaf off the tree. Difficult memories often stay with us longer than positive ones do. Although light casts out darkness a candle must be lit for the light to do its work.

Sadness can feel dark. Feelings of depression naturally accompany death. It is important to allow yourself to feel those deep feelings of grief. Sometimes when the difficult feelings linger on or the cloud of loss does not lift it can lead to despair. Despair can feel desperate, all encompassing, and hopeless. The Bible has something to say about despair. In the *Old Testament*, Isaiah speaks of God's provision for those who grieve in Zion:

to bestow on them a crown of beauty
 instead of ashes,
the oil of joy
 instead of mourning,
and a garment of praise
 instead of a spirit of despair.

This is a promise which in the midst of the feelings of despair can seem elusive. Isaiah goes on to say:

They will be called oaks of righteousness,
 a planting of the LORD
 for the display of his splendor.
– Isaiah 61:3

What grand hope that Creator God would describe His grieving people as oaks of righteousness! The oak tree is sturdy, firm, planted, and endures the harshness of the seasons, even the season of death.

God knew His people would need the inspiration of the grandeur of an oak tree as they sought to follow after Him. A legend in the faith, the Apostle Paul, writes about despair in his letter to the Corinthians. Paul is encouraging the Corinthian Christians during a time when they intimately understood the despair that comes from torture under tyrannical rule. Paul himself was beaten beyond recognition and imprisoned. He wrote of feeling like his body could not go on and described his hopeful spirit longing to honor Jesus. Paul writes about the balance between despair and joy:

We are pressed on every side by troubles, but we are not crushed. We are perplexed, but not driven to despair. We are hunted down, but never abandoned by God. We get knocked down, but we are not destroyed. Through suffering, our bodies continue to share in the death of Jesus so that the life of Jesus may also be seen in our bodies...

That is why we never give up. Though our bodies are dying, our spirits are being renewed every day. For our present troubles are small and won't last very long. Yet they produce for us a glory that vastly outweighs them and will last forever! So we don't look at the troubles we can see now; rather, we fix our gaze on things that cannot be seen. For the things we see now will soon be gone, but the things we cannot see will last forever.
– 2 Corinthians 4:8-10,16-18 NLT

Paul's feeling of despair is real—just as real as our feelings of despair. Sometimes it can feel like the sadness or hardship will never pass. I believe this is why Jesus gives us a picture of Himself as the vine, and describes us as the branches. Jesus is the oak tree. He is planted and is a firm foundation. We are the branches moved by the wind and the weather. The wind can be unrelenting pressing the branch to its breaking point. The leaves change in season but we, as branches, remain connected to the trunk.

In my life loss has come in many ways, the most recent being the loss of my church. We experienced a period of stagnation and then transition after many long-term church families left. When I hear the name of our church, Fellowship, my mind rewinds to our glory days—the time when my growing family was doing life together with the growing families of my friends. Today our church is just a shell of its previous self and I realized that when I imagine health and life I see those old families joined hand-in-hand with my family. It is as though the way I have coped is to hold on to the old picture and not replace it with the current one. I need to grieve the loss of the families who have left and let go. This will allow my hands to be open for the new families God is bringing to us. It is very important for me to embrace the new reality—one that includes new faces and new families. This is all part of the acceptance process.

God designed us to dream. Don't stop imagining something beyond the present. Jesus spoke of the Kingdom to come. Part of the responsibility of Christians is to live in the light of the coming Kingdom, recognizing life on earth is not the end. When we lose hope for the future it leads to a death in the present. When a dream dies part of us dies and it is important to mourn the loss. When we cover up the mourning, numb the mourning, or avoid the hurt, we set up a landmine for ourselves. All that is unresolved will be triggered when our next loss occurs whether big or small. Our biology is connected to our spirit and we viscerally feel loss. It's not just in your head, it's real. This is why we can become emotional around the anniversary of a loss. An important nugget from this chapter is the idea that dreams die to make way for new dreams.

God has already given His people a crown. Take out your gold crown. The crown is part of being one of His children. Loss can cause the crown to be tarnished and then buried. Pick up the crown and place it back on your head. Remember who you are in context of your loss. Remember one of Jesus' greatest directives:

> ***Whoever finds their life will lose it, and whoever loses their life for my sake will find it.***
> *– Matthew 10:39*

This next activity, *My Castle*, is one of my personal favorites. There is a little bit of mystery in it. We are going to look at life as a castle. Whether you live in an apartment, a house, or a mansion, this activity provides you an imaginary palace. Walk into all the rooms, look around. Take a big breath within the castle walls. Allow yourself to see what you see, smell what you smell, taste what you taste, and feel what you feel. Today you are the ruler of your castle and you are empowered to do an inventory of how it is running.

Activity H: My Castle

This activity is an opportunity to explore your personal castle. Take some time to think about your household.

What condition is your castle in?

Is your drawbridge up or down?

Is anyone trapped in the top tower?

What's in the attic? What's in the basement?

Is there a dragon on the inside or the outside of your castle?

Is your castle at peace or under attack?

Whether your home is a mansion, an apartment, or another living space, use the castle image to create a picture of your home. Use words, colors, and symbols.

Reflect:

Jezebel goes down in history as the wife who used her influence to make her husband do more evil.

> ***There was never anyone like Ahab, who sold himself to do evil in the eyes of the L*****ORD*****, urged on by Jezebel his wife. He behaved in the vilest manner by going after idols, like the Amorites the L*****ORD*** ***drove out before Israel.***
> – *1 Kings 21:25-26*

Process:

Take a few minutes to look at your castle. What do you notice about your world as you see it today?

What type of spouse (friend) are you?

How do the words in *1 Kings 21:25-26* strike you?

Pray:

Dear Lord,

You can see my castle. You see every room. You promise that you are making a place for me with many rooms, but right now I am here in this space and in this time. Please enter my castle. Redecorate. Bring peace and order, and reign as my King. Amen

Chapter 17:

Seasons of Life

I lived in two houses while growing up. The first house had a hill in the backyard that was wooded. We could climb the hill and be lost making forts and telling stories all day. I grew up in the '70s, '80s and '90s. This was following the poor ecological habits of the '50s where people in more rural areas buried their trash. As kids we loved digging up treasure in the back yard including old tin cans and tools.

When I was 12 years old we moved to a new house with a stream that ran in the woods along the front of our property. During the last couple years before high school when I played outside, my brothers, sister, and I would build bridges out of old two-by-fours so that we could connect the fractured kingdoms and rule in harmony. As a kid I played hard. I still have the scarred up knees to prove it.

Healing at Any Age

"Play is a fun, enjoyable activity that elevates our spirits and brightens our outlook on life. It expands self-expression, self-knowledge, self-actualization, and self-efficacy. Play relieves feelings of stress and boredom, connects us to people in a positive way, stimulates creative thinking and exploration, regulates our emotions, and boosts our ego."
– Garry Landreth

There is a lot of research substantiating that play at any age is healing. I feel passionate about incorporating paper-and-pencil activities and coloring activities into my books. In my classes I bring all sorts of different mediums for attendees to use so we can tap into different parts of our brains and open ourselves up for healing. Often I am met with terrified faces when I ask class members to make things out of pipe cleaners, but once they begin to look at the colors, touch the fibers, and move the items, their faces relax and smiles emerge. There is scientific evidence that the absence of play stunts childhood development and that adult relationships fizzle when spontaneity and laughter are absent. If you skipped the coloring activities in this book because you don't "do art" or you didn't "have time" or you were "looking for the meat" I encourage you to go back and dig in. On your lunch break stop at a craft store and get colored pencils, an assortment of stickers, and if you are really daring, some die cut shapes and a glue stick. Even 20 minutes of creating will engage your whole person in a dynamic way.

Think about what play looks like for you as you travel through the stages of development. Try to recall one story from each of the stages listed below. Life's path is a very interesting process.

Early Childhood

Infancy and Early Childhood is birth to age 5. This is a time of rapid growth in all quadrants of the person—physical, emotional, educational. Children develop from dependence to semi-independence as we venture to school and the first social separation from our parents around age 4 or 5. If you take your child to the pediatrician each year she will give you a list of the expected milestones for your child that year. At the beginning of each elementary year of school, educators give out fact sheets listing the educational expectations for how your child should be performing and what to expect from the coming year.

Trauma during this phase of development is often difficult to treat. Infant mental health research indicates that trauma that occurs when a baby is pre-lingual becomes trapped in the cells of the body and can be triggered through sounds and smells. Because the neuro development was not verbal during the abuse, there are simply no words to describe the tragic events.

I don't remember a lot from between birth to age 5. I wish I could. I know I was securely attached to my mother as she was my primary caregiver, giving up her career as a teacher to care for me. My mother read stories to me and my siblings every night. We were able to choose one library book and one Arch book which were short rhyming Bible stories. I vaguely remember the wooden paneled bedroom and the strong pitch of the roof above the twin bed. I remember my mother reading a story about the disciples and how Jesus cooked fish over the fire and asked them to be fishers of men. I can see the illustration clearly in my mind's eye. Jesus face was warm and his hands were open as the words read: *Come*. The rest of the story is legend. My mom shares that she asked every night if we wanted to trust Jesus as our personal Savior. One night I said yes and at four years and six months old I began a journey with Jesus that continues to this day.

Childhood and Adolescence

Childhood and adolescence occurs from age 6 to 20. This is a time of growth and development that includes learning social norms, understanding the world around you, and beginning to achieve. The body and mind continue to grow and emotional development begins to be challenged. Neuro pathways form connecting experience and memory to emotions. Research indicates that deprivation or neglect has even more significant consequences than physical abuse during early childhood through adolescence. When a child does not feel safe and secure, and that his day-to-day needs of food, water, shelter, and love will be met, the biology screams out for ways to self-comfort. As research expands it has been discovered that when children have their amygdala engaged the body responds emotionally—whether the child has words or not, the body takes over with a fight, flight, or freeze response that supersedes written communication.

I was a reserved and shy child. I felt very insecure. Childhood was more difficult for me because of my personality. I remember sitting on the school bus feeling scared and alone. I met one girl who talked to me. Her name was Linda Kingston but when I told my mom about my friend all I could remember was Linda King. She became a very good friend for me. Unfortunately our school district decided to redistrict, reassigning addresses to new elementary schools and for some reason our home was changed three times during those early school years. I went to the Round School for Kindergarten, the Yellow School for first grade, the Woodbridge School for second grade, and back to the Round School for third grade. In fourth grade my parents decided to enroll all of us kids in a private Christian school where I stayed until seventh grade.

The Christian school was a time of safety, security, and flourishing. I did well academically and had a few very good friends. Unfortunately the transition from elementary school to middle school was traumatic. I started the Georgetown Junior Senior High School at the time when the entire school was integrated. As a naive seventh grader, I had woodworking class with seniors. I remember feeling very afraid. One of the fears that kept me up at night was the fear of someone dealing drugs in front of my locker. I left a sheltered lily-white environment to discover teenagers smoking in the bathroom. For the first month of seventh grade I ate lunch in the library and cried myself to sleep at night. In contrast, the weekends were great. Each Friday night through Sunday morning was wonderful until the dread of returning to school descended on me like a dark cloud. Sometime after church on Sunday, I felt miserable. My misery lasted until I woke up Monday morning and made myself go to school again. Fortunately I did finally assimilate mid-year. In my eighth grade year the school district created a middle school wing so that all the locker bays and classrooms were contained on one floor. Although I would never say my years in high school were the best years of my life, I made great friends my junior and senior years. I truly enjoyed being in our senior class play. I was the president of our little chapter of the American Field Service and inducted into the National Honor Society. I was also voted best actor and friendliest by my class. Little did those other students know what a big risk it had been for me to be friendly.

Early Adulthood

Early adulthood is between 20 and 40 years old. During this time the young adult begins to differentiate from his family of origin and form his own path. As he gets a job, finds a mate, and sets goals, he enters a time of intense social growth and a season of independence. This is a time when a person often finds himself and establishes his own identity apart from the family he grew up with. The new family patterns established are very much based in his experience. Behavioral patterns with friends, partners, and co-workers are a direct reaction to what was modeled— either a compliance with the pattern or a defiant over throw of the pattern. Unprocessed trauma can result in his developing unhealthy coping methods to address unresolved hurts.

My college years were the best. I finally discovered my tribe. I attended a small liberal arts Christian college, Gordon College, where I met friends that I still have today. During these years I did a lot of self-discovery and found my calling in social work. I learned to listen well and received a solid Biblical foundation from which I still practice today. After college I moved to Louisville, Kentucky where I attended seminary and received my Master's of Social Work. While there I met another group of lifelong friends and was introduced to my husband. My late 20s and early 30s were marked by having children and raising our family. During this time life was full of adventure and dream fulfillment.

Middle Adulthood

Middle adulthood is from 40 to 60 years old. During these years adults continue to raise their children and send them off into the world. This stage can be a time when adults become concerned with creating a legacy for the next generation. After living life a certain way we may change course and set new personal goals for achievement realizing what we previously thought was important may not be as valuable as we once thought. It is often during this time when adults have a mid-life crisis. I believe this correlates with the autumn season—recognizing mistakes and missed opportunities. There is often a sense of disillusionment or disenchantment with the way life is turning out. The dream does not correlate with the reality. The breakdown may be small or big, but it is triggered by the schism between what was hoped for and what was actually achieved. An individual's dream collides with reality and often the tools used to suppress painful memories are worn down. Or maybe it is like water cresting a levy. There are finally too many unresolved feelings and experiences to keep her from rushing in. For instance, an individual's ability to keep her alcohol use (numbing) in check and maintain her job responsibilities may wane, while the intensity of parenting and the weight of family responsibility often become overwhelming. There is not enough left in the tank to keep going.

This is the stage of life where I find myself right now. It is getting better as I move through the end of this decade but I found the beginning of my 40s difficult. I experienced a collision between the dream I had for my life and the reality of where God had me. My children are older and I have new responsibilities. I no longer tie shoes and play pretend. Now, we read books and discuss big life experiences like new school policies which include holding the students in their classrooms to protect them from intruders. After 20 years of marriage the newness has worn off but there is a sense of predictability and an abiding love. Our relationship has a strong foundation and it is not going anywhere.

Late Adulthood

Finally in late adulthood which is 60 years and older, individuals may now focus on implementing legacy plans. We move into a new phase that no longer includes full time work and establishes pathways to see work continue beyond our earthly lives. This time can be marked with health issues and the deterioration or wear and tear of the physical body. During this phase individuals often evaluate what is left and what we will leave behind. Depending upon one's resilience he/she may choose to change and chart a new course. Or it can be an emotional time marked by guilt and regret. There is a sense that death is coming.

I am not at this stage of development yet but I am walking into this stage with my parents. Having watched my parents lovingly and tirelessly care for my grandparents during the end of their lives we are thinking and talking about what that next phase may look like for all of us. As for today we relish that my parents are self-sufficient, driving, and enjoying all their faculties. The reality of this stage looms before us as we know what is coming: decline, illness, and death.

The end of life can come at any stage of life, although most of us hope that death will come at the end of a full life including the raising of children and enjoyment of grandchildren. The Bible says that death comes as a thief in the night. We really can't predict it. Despite the inevitable call of death we can seize the day and enjoy the life we have.

Where We Find Ourselves on the Path

Identifying gains and losses in life can be healthy during any season of life. It is never too early to develop good emotional processing and coping skills. It is also never too late to walk through your wounding and find resolve, peace, and acceptance. If you are a parent who has tried to change unhealthy family patterns for the next generation don't lose heart. Every little change you make will influence the next generation.

We have no way of knowing what kind of, if any, self-reflection Jezebel did. We can't know if she had toys or the opportunity to play in the palace. We don't know if her mother read to her at night. We don't know what coping skills were modeled to her. Yet, we know one thing for certain—she did not adopt a spirit of play or a mechanism for self-reflection during adulthood. The Biblical narrative depicts no alteration from her course of action during the years of her rule. Her bitterness turned to hard heartedness. She had a bent toward revenge, becoming more and more violent and insolent in her old age.

At the beginning of this chapter I wrote about the power of play. Art, journaling, play, talk therapy, and education are all part of *our work*. Jezebel chose to not do *her work* and that choice left her with a legendary reputation. We have choice. We can allow the injuries from any one of our life stages to solidify into bitterness and produce a life of self-centered revenge or we can identify our injuries—and bathe them in God's myrrh which cleans deeply and heals our wounds from the inside out. It seems appropriate that the tree which has brought us rest will now bring us healing. Trees must be tapped to produce the sap or resign that will be turned into the oil we know as myrrh. So, our broom tree will be tapped to reveal even deeper healing properties.

When I began writing this part of my story I was in winter. I felt the weight of the world on my shoulders. I didn't see a way out. I could remember what spring felt like but it seemed illusive—a faint memory. As uncomfortable as it was, I needed to be in winter both weather wise and heart wise. I needed to hibernate and retreat so that I would reflect on my life. I needed the cold so that I would move toward the warmth. Do you feel stuck in any one season? As was true with Elijah it is important to feel what we feel and be in the season we are in while we are in it. God didn't leave Elijah in his difficult season too long. The model holds true for us—God won't leave us in winter too long. The beauty from Elijah's story is that a broom tree is always waiting for our exhausted, disillusioned, questioning selves. God is waiting to give us rest.

As you begin to process the challenging parts of your story don't be surprised that more and more of your story will be revealed. In fact, our memory is self-protective and often hides thoughts and feelings from us when it feels we can't handle them. It is easy to dwell on the negative emotional experiences and allow those memories to cloud or over power the greater story. As you embark on the *My Life Path* activity remember the good as well as the bad. You may be surprised to find more positive points on your path than you expect. Take time to celebrate the many beautiful gifts God has given you.

Activity I: My Life Path

Below is a picture of a stone path. This activity is the first step toward becoming unstuck. Organize your life highlights and lowlights here:

Just hang for a few minutes with your picture. Take a little time to look at it.

Next, add some insights to your journey:
- Use colored pencils or markers to depict where you were stuck, growing, or soaring.

If you have stickers do the following:
- Add a bird sticker to denote where you were soaring.
- Add a tree sticker to denote where you were growing.
- Add a skull sticker to denote places of death or loss.
- Add a star sticker to denote places that are unresolved.

Reflect:

In the thirty-eighth year of Asa king of Judah, Ahab son of Omri became king of Israel, and he reigned in Samaria over Israel twenty-two years. Ahab son of Omri did more evil in the eyes of the LORD than any of those before him. He not only considered it trivial to commit the sins of Jeroboam son of Nebat, but he also married Jezebel daughter of Ethbaal king of the Sidonians, and began to serve Baal and worship him. He set up an altar for Baal in the temple of Baal that he built in Samaria. Ahab also made an Asherah pole and did more to arouse the anger of the LORD, the God of Israel, than did all the kings of Israel before him.

In Ahab's time, Hiel of Bethel rebuilt Jericho. He laid its foundations at the cost of his firstborn son Abiram, and he set up its gates at the cost of his youngest son Segub, in accordance with the word of the LORD spoken by Joshua son of Nun.
– *1 Kings 16:29-34*

So Jezebel sent a messenger to Elijah to say, "May the gods deal with me, be it ever so severely, if by this time tomorrow I do not make your life like that of one of them."
– *1 Kings 19:2*

Process:
Use this space to process where you find yourself in the seasons of life. What stage of life are you in?
- Adolescence (<20)
- Early Adulthood (20-40)
- Middle Adulthood (40-60)
- Late Adulthood (60+)

Did you identify that you were stuck anywhere along your path?

Pray:
Dear Lord,

Thank you for my path. Thank you for the courage to look at my path. Please pour your myrrh over the broken stones which represent the heartache and suffering in my story. I love you, Jesus. Amen

Chapter 18:

Seasons and Your Tree

My best friend from college had a round silver medallion of the giving tree that she always wore on a chain around her neck. I remember being mesmerized by its delicate silver filigree. I enjoyed looking at it. It's been years since college and I never asked her the story behind the necklace. While writing this book I asked her about the pendant. She told me that very close family friends had given it to her as a present when she graduated from high school. She says she treasures the necklace because it was a gift from her favorite science teacher (even though physics was one of her worst classes). She also shared that it reminded her that she was created for abundant life. It represents an image of God as *provider who gives everything that is necessary for her and all of us to "live well" and live for His glory.*

Throughout this book we have explored the life cycle of a leaf. When I first began my research I was shocked by how the journey of a leaf mirrored the journey of life. The leaf cannot survive apart from the tree. God created the leaf and tree to be connected. Jesus said: *I am the tree and you are the branches. You cannot live apart from me.*

We learned that when an oak tree stops providing nourishment to its leaves it is only a matter of time before the leaves die. We understand that trees are rooted to withstand storms, scorching heat, dry ground, and floods. We discovered that trees have a long lifespan. Jesus likening Himself to a tree gives us a powerful picture of His character. The interconnectedness of the leaf to the branch to the tree is a creative marvel.

Peter Wohlleben is an arborist. He has committed his life to the protection of trees as a forester and shares many mysterious and wonderful truths about trees in his book, *The Hidden Life of Trees: What They Feel, How They Communicate.* I won't lie; I bought the book based on the title and the cover art. I knew nothing of Peter before I read the book. I saw the title on Amazon and hoped the book might shed light on the emotional life of a tree. The cover art captured an image of three beautiful trees with their roots interconnected under the ground. With my fascination with trees and my desire to use the tree as an illustration for this book, I thought: *this is a must read!*

Much of the book was a cross between lessons in photosynthesis and carbon dating. The science went a bit over my head but I was determined to find something that made the image on the cover make sense and I slogged through it. The entire book was worth reading for one chapter called *Friendship*. Wohlleben explains that while walking in the woods he discovered what he thought was a large moss-covered rock. After exploring the mass he discovered that it was actually an old tree stump. The properties of the stump baffled him because the stump appeared to still be alive. This made no sense as common knowledge tells that when you chop down a tree it dies. What he discovered was fascinating. Trees of the same species connect with one another underground. The roots tangle and twist far beneath the earth and they exchange nutrients to keep one another alive. So, forests are actually groups of friends nurturing and protecting one another. Although the tree trunk is severed from its leafy canopy, the tree friends continue to support each other long after the tree has been felled.

While the leaf has a distinct life cycle typically lasting one year, a tree can live thousands of years. As we know now trees live in community. The Creator of the universe understands the dynamic life of His creation whether trees or people. Jesus used the tree as a symbol of interconnectedness between He and His people. His design for community surpasses what we will ever understand during our mortal lives. This design is woven through each part of the created order. How do seasons affect the trees? Nature's elements are hard: rain, wind, snow, and temperature. The change of seasons can be harsh and God designed trees to stand together and withstand whatever is thrown at them.
God's people can learn from the lives of trees. By connecting deeply underground, relying on the One True tree, we can literally weather all the stages of our lives together.

A few years ago I received a piece of wall art from a friend. She gave it to me because it was a tree painting that looked similar to the broom tree. We hung the painting above our coat rack in the front entryway. A poem written by Bonnie L. Mohr was printed under the tree image. The script was small and we hung the picture so high no one could really read it. I only read the entire poem twice. First, after I unwrapped it when receiving it as a gift and again during the writing of this chapter when I dug it out of a closet and laid it on our kitchen table.

Living Life
Bonnie L. Mohr

Life is not a race – but indeed a journey.
Be honest. Work hard. Be choosy.
Say "thank you," "I love you," and "great job"
to someone each day.
Go to church, take time for prayer.
The Lord giveth and the Lord taketh.
Let your handshake mean more than pen and paper. Love your life and what you've been given,
it is not accidental – search for your purpose and
do it as best you can.
Dreaming does matter. It allows you to become
that which you aspire to be.
Laugh often.
Appreciate the little things in life and enjoy them.
Some of the best things really are free.
Do not worry, less wrinkles are more becoming.
Forgive, it frees the soul.
Take time for yourself – plan for longevity.
Recognize the special people you've
been blessed to know.
Live for today, enjoy the moment.

As I read these words I thought to myself, *what a shame it was up so high and out of sight. If only I had hung it lower where I could read it regularly and remember.* I imagined where I could hang it so that I could now think of the great advice every day. Mohr says: *Dreaming does matter!* When I think of how often my dreaming was stopped by heart ache, pain, and betrayal over the past five years it makes my heart hurt. For a season the picture was hung too high to read. All I saw was the picture of the tree which reminded me to embrace God's rest. Now for this season the picture reminds me to rest so that I continue to dream.

Many other famous writers have told the story of the tree. Most notably, Shel Silverstein wrote a beautiful book called *The Giving Tree*. It takes the reader on a whimsical journey of the life of a tree. From the place a child once climbed and hung to swing from its branches to the tree's sacrifice for what the young man needed in his life. In the final phase of life the tree offered all it had left, its stump for the now old man to rest on.

There is similar folktale retold by Angela Hunt called *The Tale of Three Trees*. The story is about three trees imagining what they will do with their lives. They are each planted in different places. They each face different challenges as they grow. And they each have great dreams for their lives. The one tree imagines she will be carved into a beautiful trunk one day and hold precious items. The next imagines he will be a great sailing vessel. The last hopes she will be the beam that holds up a great building. Each of the trees is transformed into an important item. The first is fashioned into a manger that later holds the baby Jesus. The wood from the second tree is used to build a simple but sturdy fishing boat—the boat the disciples fished from and Jesus taught from. Finally the last tree was made into great beams, one that Jesus struggled to carry up the hill of Golgotha and that he was later crucified on.

This old tale reminds us to look beyond what we can see in our own story. It encourages us to widen our vision and think of the greater narrative. God is beyond time and is sovereign over the cosmic story. The simple legend of the three trees can help us gain perspective and enlarge our vision of the broom tree concept.

The Bible uses trees as metaphors for His plans and purposes. Adam and Eve were given responsibility to tend the trees and cautioned to not touch the tree of good and evil. Jesus called Himself the vine and His people the branches. Jonah had a tree grow up over him while he waited on God to destroy Nineveh. Elijah hid under the broom tree where God gave him nourishment and rest. Isaiah encourages the people that they can be oaks of righteousness by living lives of faithfulness. The image of the tree is powerful and encouraging.

What would a tree of righteousness look like? What does your tree look like? Has it been alone on a prairie or is it in a forest side-by-side with others of its kind? Are your leaves a vibrant green, yellow, or brown? Does your tree have leaves or is it naked as it hibernates, waiting for new life?

This activity is an opportunity to take time to celebrate. Take a few moments to think about your favorite season. Why is Spring, Summer, Fall, or Winter your favorite? What do you like about that particular season? What are your best memories from that season? This activity provides a space to process your feelings about all the seasons as you select your favorite. Hopefully this exercise will provide you with emotional air helping you to identify where your dream may be stuck in one season or the other.

Activity J: My Favorite Season

What is your favorite season of the year? Use the tree on the next page to depict that favorite season.

Reflect:
> *He has sent me to bind up the brokenhearted,*
> > *to proclaim freedom for the captives*
> > *and release from darkness for the prisoners,*
> *to proclaim the year of the Lord's favor*
> > *and the day of vengeance of our God,*
> *to comfort all who mourn,*
> > *and provide for those who grieve in Zion—*
> *to bestow on them a crown of beauty*
> > *instead of ashes,*
> *the oil of joy*
> > *instead of mourning,*
> *and a garment of praise*
> > *instead of a spirit of despair.*
> *They will be called oaks of righteousness,*
> > *a planting of the Lord for display of his splendor.*
> – Isaiah 61:1-3

This Scripture in *Isaiah* has powerful images that help us to visualize God's renewal and the healing of His people. Consider returning to this entire chapter of Scripture for further reflection.

Process:

Why is this your favorite season?

What did you experience during this season?

What memories make this your favorite time of the year?

How does your experience with this season fit with the actual, natural season of the year?

Pray:
　Dear God,
　Please bind up my broken heart and remind me of the freedom I have in you. Amen.

Chapter 19:

Seasons of Reflection

My dad, Bill Boylan, grew up in a small New England town post World War II. My grandfather, Vincent (Vince), grew up in that same town with a grandfather who struggled with alcohol rage, money management issues, and virtually void of God. Long before my father was born, my father's Great Aunt Mae began piano lessons. At the time the Boylan's were practicing Roman Catholics. One day the nuns decided to give Mae an unused piano from the rectory. My father's great grandfather Tom Boylan went to the church and brought it home. One can only imagine the physical stress of transporting a piano without a dolly or pick-up truck. Sometime after the piano was moved in and set up; the priest learned of the gift. He stormed off to the Boylan's home and planned to take the piano back to the church. Only the priest met his match with Tom; he was not going to let the piano go. A great argument ensued and in the end the priest returned pianoless to the church.

Tom Boylan did not attend church that next Sunday. According to the legend recounted to Tom by his friends, the priest announced to the congregation that Tom had failed to obey his order to return the piano and pronounced a Black Mass to ask God to turn Tom into *the snake that he was*. From that time on the Boylan family ceased being Roman Catholic and Tom ended his faith all together.

When my grandparents Vince Boylan and Annie Brown got married in 1938, they used the parsonage of the Congregational Church for their ceremony. Arthur (Vince's father, my grandfather) stood up for the groom while Gladys (Anne's sister, my grammy) stood up for the bride. It is wondered if my grandparents chose the parsonage because it was a location outside of the church and that way Arthur would attend.

Arthur's first wife, Ethelyn, died shortly before Vince and Anne married. It is also wondered if cupid's arrow may have struck Arthur and Gladys at my grandparents' wedding, because not long after, they too were married—leading to my dad's aunt becoming his grandmother.

Arthur and Gladys built a house and their yard became my dad's playground. One spring day Gladys was finally able to drag Arthur with her to the local Baptist Church. My dad accompanied them to church to hear Reverend Spaulding preach. After church they all returned home and Gladys began cooking hamburgers. It has been a long time since that day in the early '40s but my dad says he can still remember how the hamburgers tasted. While Gladys cooked those memorable burgers, Arthur sternly summoned my dad to follow him out behind the chicken coop. My dad says his stomach dropped as he questioned what he had done wrong and why he might be getting into trouble. Out behind the chicken coop Arthur ranted about the sermon specifically arguing against the virgin birth. This was one of the few theological lessons my dad received from his grandfather.

Beyond religion there was a tradition of violence in the Boylan family. As a child Vince lived with his parents Arthur and Ethelyn Boylan and his maternal grandfather Willard Harris. Vince was close to and loved his paternal grandfather (my great grandfather) Willard. Unfortunately he feared with good reason his maternal grandfather Tom. Most days Vince would walk home from his neighborhood school, eat a snack, and hop the fence to play with his friends in the playground. If all went well, he played until he was called home for supper. But the afternoons when his grandfather Tom finished work early did not go well. A stone mason, Tom worked hard and drank even harder. On shortened workdays, Tom started drinking early. On those days Tom would look for Vince, take him home, sit him down at the table, and force feed him liver and onions. My dad remembers Vince sharing stories of how he desperately hoped his father would come home and rescue him, but it seldom happened.

Not only did Vince never forget the feeling of being forced to eat liver, he also never forgot that Tom died while under the influence the alcohol. Mary Olmstead was Tom Boylan's wife and my great-great grandmother. After putting up with years of drinking and irresponsible behavior, Mary left Tom. She also left Ipswich and moved to a neighboring town called Salem. One night in the middle of a raging blizzard a drunken Tom decided to walk ten miles and bring back his wife. Needless to say when he returned wifeless from his hike he was wet and cold. His cold developed into pneumonia and he later died. Although it was never said out loud, my dad has the distinct sense that Vince did not want to end up like his father and swore off alcohol. My dad recounts: *anyone who opened our kitchen cabinet might have imagined that we were planning to open a liquor store.* The cabinet was packed with unopened bottles of liquor. Vince drove a truck for The Railway Express Agency and was well liked and highly respected. During the holidays, business owners would give him a fifth as a gift. Vince would accept the gift and immediately put it away in that cabinet.

My grandfather was raised by a father and influenced by a grandfather who believed that honor was achieved through brute force. Tom was raised by an alcoholic and had a very strict older brother. One of the family's famed old stories is about Tom Boylan's older brother. It explains a lot about how the family came to value strength and never-say-die toughness. Tom's brother owned a cargo ship and sailed back and forth across the North Atlantic and over the Great Banks. It was a dangerous business and he absolutely forbade having rum on board. The last thing he wanted when far out to sea was a drunken crew. The crew had other ideas. Sometime around 1866 Tom was made a deckhand. Young and vulnerable to pressure, he succumbed to the insistence of the crew and brought rum aboard.

About mid-way in the journey from Digby, Novia Scotia, Tom's brother discovered what Tom had done. The punishment was severe. Tom was keel-hauled. He was tied with a rope, thrown overboard, and dragged the length of the ship, under the keel, and pulled up on the other side. If anything went wrong he could have died. One can only imagine the terror of such an experience. Once thrown overboard, Tom helplessly sank into frigid North Atlantic waters and banged up against the barnacle-covered hull. He fought to hold his breath long enough to make it to the other side. This helps explain how Tom was toughened. It also explains how Tom could have treated Arthur so cruelly one snowy night.

Another story recounts a wintry night when the snow was piling up fast. A ten-year-old Arthur drove with Tom to downtown Ipswich in a buckboard. The year was about 1899. Horses were the mode of transportation; automobiles were only for the wealthy. On the way back home as they crossed the railroad tracks Tom said something to Arthur to which he sassed a response. Without a word Tom swung his arm, hit his son up-side the head, snapped the reins, and drove three miles back home without his boy. Arthur walked all the way home as temperatures dropped and the wind piled up the snow. These stories offer great examples of how fear, violence, and alcohol were a normal part of my family history.

Every family has these types of stories and it can be very easy to dwell on the negative family patterns. So, while researching for this chapter, I asked my dad if he had any stories that depicted how our family patterns had changed for the better. He shared that his father Vince not only changed the family history of alcoholism but also became known for great kindness. He modeled empathetic respect to my father who shared that example with me.

My dad is a great athlete. From eighth grade to his junior year of high school his football team was undefeated. He was voted captain of the football team when he was in eleventh grade. He doesn't play football anymore but he continues to win the Senior Olympic golf tournaments all over New England.

Back in high school, my dad was in great shape. He was strong and fearless. Why Billy Davis, *the wise guy* of school thought he should pick on my dad is still a mystery. It was math class and Billy sat behind my dad. Billy was a senior. He was tall and lanky and more impressed with himself than he deserved. Although the details are fuzzy now, my dad thinks Billy made fun of a hole in his t-shirt. My dad felt embarrassed most likely because he was trying to impress a girl. Whatever the reason, he was thoroughly humiliated and that shame ignited his anger.

By the time class ended my dad had simmered down but when he left class Billy continued to taunt him in the hallway. When Billy made fun of him again my dad spun around (almost to his own surprise), grabbed Billy's shirt under his chin, drove an elbow into his ribcage, and pressed Billy's nose up against his own. It happened so fast Billy didn't know what hit him. My dad held him up with his left arm and walked with him to the top of the stairs. They stopped at a classroom door with windows reinforced with wire between the panes. With one arm my dad drove Billy into the door. When he bounced back, he hit him with one punch driving him back into the window pane again. Stunned, Billy slid down the door until he landed in a heap on the floor. That one punch was the extent of the fight.

Mr. Colby, the science teacher and assistant football coach, was the monitor in the upstairs corridor that day. He reacted as quickly as he could. He grabbed my dad's arm and whisked him away into his lab. *Sit down,* he ordered. *Cool off,* he demanded. My dad eventually cooled off and went back to class. Mr. Colby handled the skirmish *old school*. His stern reprimand was enough; no need to summon the principal or call my dad's parents. In fact the science teacher didn't report anything about the incident.

But as often happens in a small town, news traveled fast. When my dad returned home after school his grandfather Arthur met him at the door. Arthur's face was beaming and he shook my dad's hand heartily. Much to my dad's surprise Arthur congratulated him on punching the other student's lights out. To this day my dad never remembers his grandfather congratulating him for anything else. This of course was quite contrary to his own father's values. Vince was not thrilled and he scolded my dad, teaching him that violence was not the answer.

My dad had two distinct models for conflict management. His grandfather and great-grandfather lived by the philosophy that *might makes right*. His father on the other hand lived by the principle *turn the other cheek*. Vince Boylan dramatically changed the culture of our family. He embodied unconditional love. He demonstrated grace, mercy, and compassion toward everyone he met and was known in Ipswich as a kind man. Unlike Arthur and Tom who found honor through intimidation, Vince displayed genuine care and empathy toward others. He shone a light on right living and my father brought that way to me. In 1959 while in the army my father was saved by Jesus Christ. The loving model of his father coupled with the radical teachings of Jesus changed the course of our family forever. Vince made an earthly difference. Jesus made an eternal one.

My Dad's Kingdom

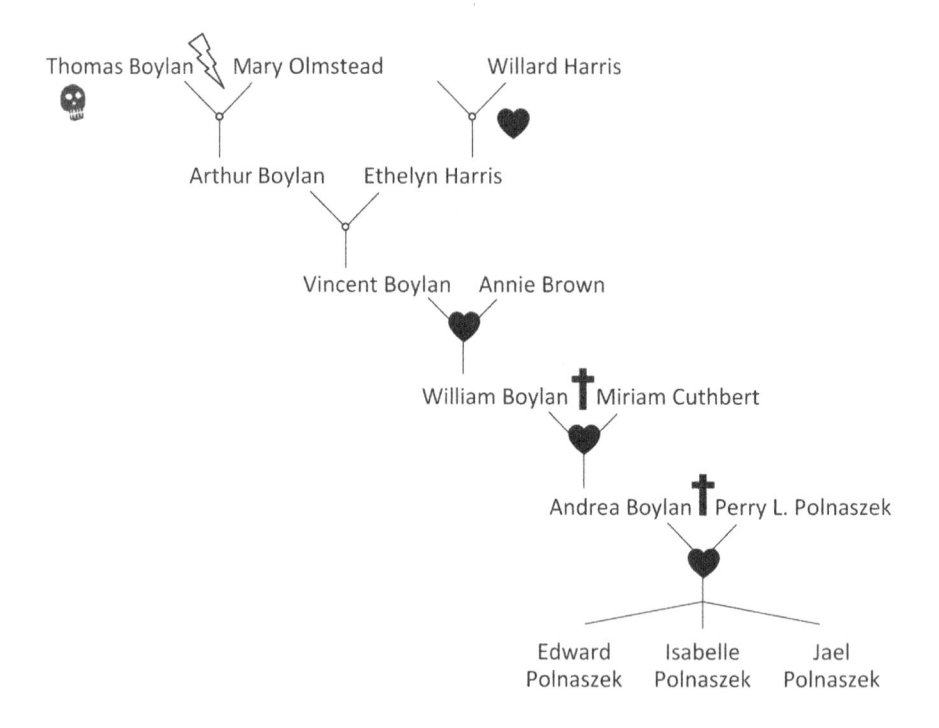

```
Thomas Boylan ⚡ Mary Olmstead        Willard Harris
     💀         \   /                      \  /
                 Y                          ♥
                 |                          |
           Arthur Boylan              Ethelyn Harris
                   \                    /
                    \                  /
                     Y
                     |
              Vincent Boylan   Annie Brown
                         \    /
                          ♥
                          |
                  William Boylan ✝ Miriam Cuthbert
                              ♥
                              |
                       Andrea Boylan ✝ Perry L. Polnaszek
                                   ♥
                         _____|_____
                         |         |         |
                      Edward    Isabelle    Jael
                     Polnaszek  Polnaszek  Polnaszek
```

This is a mini-picture of my father's side of the family.

Like my family every family has change makers. Whether for the good or the bad family members make decisions that affect the next generation. Jezebel married into a family of renown. Ahab was the son of Omri. The Bible notes that Omri did worse in the eyes of the Lord than Jeraboam who had made a way for idol worship in the Northern Kingdom of Israel. The historical trajectory is staggering. From a worldly perspective, Omri did many great things for Israel. He bought a piece of land called Samaria and moved the capital there. His military feats brought peace and prosperity to the land. Omri ushered in the longest consistent reign of Northern Kingdom leaders. Fifty years span between himself, his son Ahab, and Ahab's son Joram. But although the kingdom had grown, from God's perspective the people had been led far from Him. All throughout the *Old Testament* God had warned the Israelites not to marry women outside of the kingdom. He had warned against intermarriage because when people from other tribes came together they brought with them the worship of idols and other gods. Omri made it permissible to worship other gods. In fact he encouraged it. Like the Bible says: *He did worse in the eyes of the* Lord *than his forefather Jeroboam.* And then the Bible says: *Ahab did worse than his father.*

As we explored earlier, Omri and Ethbaal arranged the marriage between Ahab and Jezebel to bring peace and prosperity to their lands. She took worship of the pantheon to a whole new level. She not only tolerated but encouraged it by adding statues of Baal and Asherah poles right alongside the worship centers for the God of Abraham, Isaac and Jacob. She killed God's priests and publicly mocked the prophet Elijah.

Ahab took the family curse and made it worse. He solidified the ugly and praised the grotesque. He did the opposite of what we commonly think of as breaking the family curse. He went down in history as the worst not the best. And likewise Jezebel is cited as leading her husband down the path—*as encouraged by his wife Jezebel.* She used her influence to encourage the degradation of the culture Abraham had established and Noah had lived by so many years before. We can imagine how Jezebel was rewarded for doing evil and became desensitized to violence and cruelty. It is important to see that she did not operate in a vacuum. She was part of a family system and the choices of both her parents and her husband's parents affected her political career. Jezebel was warned. She is an adult woman at the time of Elijah's prophesy. This means she can think for herself and make her own choices. She chose to not listen, not heed, and perpetuate the life she had known.

Jezebel and Ahab's Kingdom

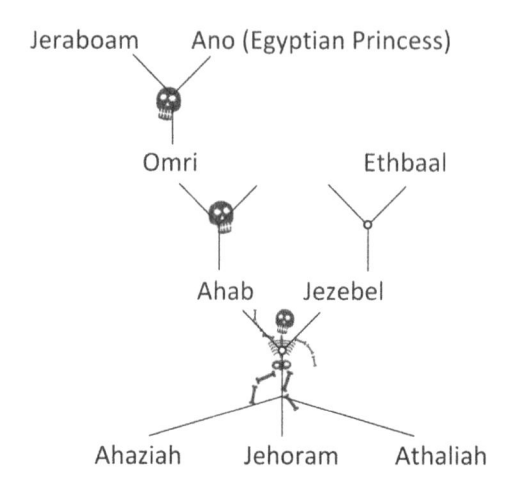

```
Jeraboam    Ano (Egyptian Princess)
        \  /
         ☠
         |
       Omri            Ethbaal
         \              /
          ☠            ○
          |            |
        Ahab        Jezebel
            \       /
              ☠
           / | \
          /  |  \
    Ahaziah Jehoram Athaliah
```

In graduate school I was introduced to a concept that gave me a new vision for family patterns, traits, and generational tendencies. The mapping tool is called a genogram. A genogram is an emotional and psychological roadmap for the family. The process is simple but not easy. The essential book for understanding genograms was written by Monica McGoldrick, Randy Gerson, and Sueli Petry. It is over 300 pages long and includes a thorough explanation of how genograms work. It is a wonderful clinical tool, however the data collection and process to plot the information is intense. With the dawn of the internet there are sophisticated computer programs that make the diagramming more streamlined but the process is still time consuming. If you enjoy genealogy and have the time, I encourage you to learn more about genograms and complete the authentic program. It is very worthwhile.

For the sake of *The Elijah Project 2, A New Season* I am going to simplify and offer an abridged tool to take advantage of the power of the exercise but not require the same intensity of information or time to complete.

I have created a simple lattice work that will allow you to map your family history including behavioral, educational, and spiritual patterns. There are two examples included in this chapter, one for my father's side of our family and one for Omri. Like the examples from my family and Jezebel's, you can plot your family patterns as well. This activity may take some time. Use a pencil and jot down what you know and then use what you don't know as a launch pad to ask other family members what they know.

Activity K: My Kingdom
- Start with yourself on the bottom of the page.
- Connect yourself to your spouse and list your children.
- Then, go two generations back, connecting everyone with a single line.
- Next, identify your family traits with colors and symbols.

These are suggestions; add colors and symbols for other family traits that are present in your family.

Red = anger
Orange = an ism (alcoholism, drug abuse, codependency, addiction)
Blue = depression or mental illness
Single hash mark = divorce
Double hash mark = death
Pink = joy, happiness
Green = peace, growth
Cross = faith-filled relationship

Reflect:

"[God] says, 'I am going to bring disaster on you. I will wipe out all your descendants and cut off from Ahab every last male in Israel—slave or free. I will make your house like that of Jeroboam son of Nebat and that of Baasha son of Ahijah, because you have aroused my anger and have caused Israel to sin.'

"And also concerning Jezebel the LORD says: 'Dogs will devour Jezebel by the wall of Jezreel. Dogs will eat those belonging to Ahab who die in the city, and the birds will feed on those who die in the country.'"

(There was never anyone like Ahab, who sold himself to do evil in the eyes of the LORD, urged on by Jezebel his wife. He behaved in the vilest manner by going after idols, like the Amorites the LORD drove out before Israel.)

When Ahab heard these words, he tore his clothes, put on sackcloth and fasted. He lay in sackcloth and went around meekly.
– 1 Kings 21:21-27

He not only considered it trivial to commit the sins of Jeroboam son of Nebat, but he also married Jezebel daughter of Ethbaal king of the Sidonians, and began to serve Baal and worship him. He set up an altar for Baal in the temple of Baal that he built in Samaria. Ahab also made an Asherah pole and did more to arouse the anger of the LORD, the God of Israel, than did all the kings of Israel before him.
– 1 Kings 16:31-33

Process:

Look at the *My Kingdom* illustration. What family patterns emerge?

What bad patterns have been stopped? What good patterns have been started?

How are your emotions affecting your kingdom?

How is your faith affecting your kingdom? How is your grief affecting your kingdom?

Pray:
Dear Lord,

I am striving toward life forever in Your Kingdom, but my job is to bring Your Kingdom here on earth now. Please grant me insight and courage to make the changes that I need in order for Your light to flow from my life, my family, and my work, until You return. Amen.

Chapter 20:

The Power of Your Season

Trees have become very important to me. I love trees. Funny that this book began with the same sentiment about movies. I love movies. I should love movies about trees. I can't think of a movie that really captures the beauty, elegance, and intricacy of trees wrapped in a good story about life. The broom tree has been my mascot of sorts—a tree that offered protection, a place for reflection and divinity.

As I look back over my life I have always appreciated trees. Our wedding reception was in a barn in Modsley State Forest, October 1997. Our wedding invitations had a delicate leaf design created by a friend and our wedding program had matching art. My mom fashioned tableware by affixing perfect fall colored leaves to the bottom of clear plastic plates that our guests ate off. Our wedding day was an unseasonable 70 degrees. The fall colors were vivid. Orange, yellow, and red leaves provided a picture perfect backdrop for our wedding photography. In fact our pictures actually look like we are in front of a green screen.

Our first home was decorated with a leaf theme. We had framed tree art, leaf picture frames—we even had a beautiful green leaf patterned comforter. My husband and I were literally surrounded by foliage. As I reflect on it now I realize that our home, our relationship, and in many ways our life, was in Spring. Everything was new; we were creating a new life together full of hope and promise. For us, our first year of marriage was a honeymoon. We truly enjoyed each others' company and began an exciting adventure together. Very little was difficult during those early years. The world was our oyster and we explored, developed, and grew together.

After 15 years of marriage, three children, three churches, household moves, injuries, and death, we had moved through many seasons. Looking back I can see that the broom tree was the nexus of our journey. After years of fully living, we found ourselves needing rest. I needed rest. The bright green comforter is long gone now. Recently while cleaning out a closet I found one of the throw pillows from our duvet set and had a rush of memory back to our first home. Holding the pillow in one hand I was transported back to the upstairs apartment where we lived in one room while renovating the other rooms. I remember being snuggled under the weight of our down bedclothes imagining life as a mother after finding out I was pregnant. Our bedroom decor has had a few iterations but its current colors are red and gold. That strikes me as interesting because maybe the colors signal that we are in fall. No matter our present season, our marriage has weathered a lot of life and we are both embracing that change is a constant part of life.

Trees are as important to God as they are to me. When God created His perfect world He placed a tree in the center of the garden. It was the tree of good and evil. He warned Adam and Eve not to eat of it. God had perfect communion with His people walking in the cool of day, talking, and enjoying the world around them. We don't know how many times Satan slithered by to question Eve. We can surmise that he wore her down with questions of doubt like: *Why aren't you eating that fruit? Doesn't it look amazing? If God really loved you wouldn't He let you be like Him?*

Genesis 3 recounts that one day Eve succumbed to the questioning. She took the fruit and ate it and gave it to Adam. In that moment perfection shatters. Life in the garden radically changes; no longer were there ideal growing conditions and unhindered conversations with God. After the Fall humanity was banished from Eden. There was pain in childbirth, obstacles with work, and disconnection from God. These changes brought favorable and unfavorable growing seasons. Now the weather fluctuated region from region between extreme hot and bitter cold.

After God sent Adam and Eve from the garden He did something interesting. He guarded the entrance to the garden with flaming swords. I've always thought of this as a warning or part of His continued consequences or punishment. Almost like the old expression about a hot stove: *if you touch this, you will get burned.*

My father shared a story with me that he remembered from a Billy Graham sermon in the '60s. The legendary preacher described the flaming swords as God's perfect protection for His people. God had warned Adam and Eve that if they ate the fruit they would surely die. When the Fall actually happened, rather than killing them, God gave Adam and Eve consequences. God knew there was little room for error in this way again. If humans were to eat of the fruit again it would be the eradication of man. God guards the garden even now so that humans cannot be tempted to bring ultimate destruction upon themselves and work outside of His plan.

God uses the tree as an illustration throughout His word. The tree is a powerful image. From the tree of good and evil in the garden, to the burning bush in the wilderness, to Elijah's broom tree in the Sahara, to the wood trough Jesus was laid in after his birth, to the tree trunk Jesus carried to Golgotha for His crucifixion—the image is powerful. Christians wear small wooden crosses to this day representing His great sacrifice for our freedom. I do not claim that I understood the power of the tree image 20 years ago when I got married or that I fully comprehend all of its meaning today, but I know it provides a wonderful visual picture of God's loving protection and provision.

A rain storm recently swept through our backyard. The rain pelted the windows while the trees swayed back and forth with the force of the wind. After the rain stopped my husband and I took our dog for a walk and were greeted by a great surprise. Our backyard had a large tree lying across our clothes line with the tip of its branches just missing the roof of our house. We were spared any damage. It took a few days before we could arrange a team to remove the tree. One Saturday morning our friend came with a chain saw. First, he cut off the branches. Our family took branches with beautiful green leaves and threw them in the back of a utility truck. For hours our friend chopped while we piled. Finally the grass was visible again and the only damage was some broken clothes line.

While we piled the logs my husband noticed something funny. We all gathered around and inspected the center of the tree trunk. Along with the typical rings there was a red stain toward the center ring. The discoloration was remarkable so we investigated and found out that in fact it is called *staining* and it occurs when a certain fungus attacks the tree during its growth and development. This experience happened while I was writing this book. I found it fascinating that something that attacked the tree years ago left a distinct mark at the time of the attack. The rest of the rings are typical, beginning before the stain and radiating out after the stain. I am no arborist, but this science lesson was interesting. It made me think of the marks we receive over time in life. We grow, we are wounded, we heal, and we grow some more leaving a rich architecture in life's landscape.

My idea of the broom tree has expanded from its original vision. My understanding of the tree was so small and singular when I began *The Elijah Project* process. In *Genesis 1:12 and 29*, it says:

> *The land produced vegetation: plants bearing seed according to their kinds and trees bearing fruit with seed in it according to their kinds. And God saw that it was good.*
> *Then God said, "I give you every seed-bearing plant on the face of the whole earth and every tree that has fruit with seed in it. They will be yours for food."*

God's protection and provision for us began in the garden, was manifested through the gift of His Son, and continues today. No matter what season your tree is in there is a beauty when its colorful leaves are displayed. God desires that we find community with Him and others that allows our trees to manifest the true season we are in. When your tree is part of a grove and adorns a forest the world will see the immense beauty of God's faithfulness to His people.

I love trees and I love movies. Art often reflects life. A good movie script will follow the heroine's journey. The action and adventure ebbs and flows. A mentor is introduced. Tragedy is met with submission and in the end the heroine learns valuable life-changing lessons that we all hope she takes into her future life. As we own more and more of our own story there is an ease and comfort in living in our own skin. And as we share more of ourselves with others not only do we grow but we positively affect the lives of those around us.

There is a song in the popular 2017 musical, *The Greatest Showman* called *Come Alive*. The lyrics are a powerful charge for life, dreaming, and welcoming light into dark places. The song sums up our seasons work well.

God's redemptive hope is for each of us to accept exactly where we are today. He desires that we embrace the season we are in and allow Him to let us come alive within the reality of that season. Whether we are dreaming, developing, disillusioned, or feeling dead, God promises to enter into our pain with us. We can trust Him as our ultimate pathway to peace.

The Greatest Showman musical embodies the struggle of every one. In the story, P.T. Barnum's dream launches *The Greatest Show on Earth*. In the film version of his story he invites people with various disabilities, people who live in the shadows of society, to find a place in the world. The song *Come Alive* is a triumphant ballad that champions life. It calls all of us to invite God's loving light to flow through us and bring life and light to the world around us. As you accept the season you are in, invite God to usher you to your next season and share this process of growth with the people around you. Your story is a beautiful reflection of the powerful love of the Lord.

Come Alive

You stumble through your days
Got your head hung low
Your skies' a shade of grey
Like a zombie in a maze
You're asleep inside
But you can shake awake

'Cause you're just a dead man walking
Thinking that's your only option
But you can flip the switch and brighten up
your darkest day
Sun is up and the color's blinding
Take the world and redefine it
Leave behind your narrow mind
You'll never be the same

Come alive, come alive
Go and ride your light
Let it burn so bright
Reaching up
To the sky

And it's open wide
You're electrified

When the world becomes a fantasy
And you're more than you could ever be
'Cause you're dreaming with your eyes wide open
And you know you can't go back again
To the world that you were living in
'Cause you're dreaming with your eyes wide open
So, come alive!

I see it in your eyes
You believe that lie
That you need to hide your face
Afraid to step outside
So you lock the door
But don't you stay that way

No more living in those shadows
You and me we know how that goes

'Cause once you see it, oh you'll never, never be the same

We'll be the light that's turning
Bottle up and keep on shining

You can prove there's more to you

To anyone who's bursting with a dream

Come one! Come all!
You hear
The call

To anyone who's searching for a way to break free
Break free!

The spiritual implications of this song are overwhelming. Come one, come all as you hear the call. Come if you are searching to break free. There is no simple way to break free. We must do the hard work of owning our story in order to know who we are in the story. No matter what season you find yourself in, what developmental stage you are in, where you are on the spiritual continuum, or where you are on the journey between dreaming and death, you can COME ALIVE!

The art of acceptance hangs in the balance of the constancy of change and we are invited to walk that line. *The Serenity Prayer* by Reinhold Neihbur has been quoted by folks in recovery for many years. Most of us are familiar with the line: *grant me the serenity to accept the things I cannot change, courage to change the things I can, and wisdom to know the difference.* Later in the prayer, Neihbur writes: *Accepting hardships as the pathway to peace.* I find great solace in that stanza. There is something powerful about living in the moment rather than escaping from it. There is power when we accept how uncomfortable it is to remain our whole interconnected self in the midst of the complexity of life. It is only through this process that we have hope of true contentment.

The apostle Paul experienced great hardship, abuse, and physical persecution. He writes about finding a sense of contentment beyond his circumstances:

> ***And the <u>peace</u> of God, which transcends all <u>understanding</u>, will guard your hearts and your minds in Christ Jesus.***
> – *Philippians 4:7*

No matter the season you find yourself in, may God's peace allow you to move beyond what you can see and feel so that your heart and mind are protected by Him.

The final activity, *Bringing it All Together*, is an invitation to bring all of the ideas from *The Elijah Project 2, A New Season* together into one picture. Take a little time to assemble an image that reflects your path, your castle, and your tree to give you a snapshot into your present reality and give yourself permission to accept the reality of that story.

Activity L: Bringing It All Together

Below is a unique picture. It includes the castle with a path under a large tree. The picture offers you an opportunity to bring your entire journey together. Feel free to be creative with words, sayings, images, and colors depicting you in this season of your life. Allow the picture to reflect your past experiences and your future hopes.

Resources

Acceptance Was The Answer
Alcoholic Anonymous, *Big Book*

Let it Be
The Beatles

Youth and Age
Samuel Taylor Coleridge

The Tale of Three Trees
Angela Hunt

Play Therapy: The Art of the Relationship
Garry Landreth

Living Life
Bonnie L. Mohr

On Grief and Grieving:
Finding the Meaning of Grief Through the Five Stages of Loss
Elisabeth Kübler-Ross MD, David Kessler

The Seasons Of Life
M.S. Lowndes

Genograms: Assessment and Intervention
Monica McGoldrick, Randy Gerson PhD, Sueli Petry PhD

Come Alive
Music and Lyrics by Benj Pasek and Justin Paul

How to Recognize the Spiritual Season of Life You're In
Courtnaye Richard

The Art of Exceptional Living
Jim Rohn

The Four Seasons of Transformation
Jim Rohn

The Giving Tree
Shel Silverstein

**The Hidden Life of Trees:
What They Feel, How They Communicate**
Peter Wohlleben

Widowspeak: a Story of Grief and Joy
Renee J. Wurzer

Scripture References

All Scripture quotations, unless otherwise indicated, are taken from the Holy Bible, New International Version®, NIV®. Copyright ©1973, 1978, 1984, 2011 by Biblica, Inc.™ Used by permission of Zondervan. All rights reserved worldwide. www.zondervan.com The "NIV" and "New International Version" are trademarks registered in the United States Patent and Trademark Office by Biblica, Inc.™

Scripture quotations marked (NLT) are taken from the Holy Bible, New Living Translation, copyright ©1996, 2004, 2015 by Tyndale House Foundation. Used by permission of Tyndale House Publishers, Inc., Carol Stream, Illinois 60188. All rights reserved.

1 Kings 16:29-34
1 Kings 16:31-33
1 Kings 19:2
1 Kings 21:21-27
1 Kings 21:25-26
1 Samuel 12:14
2 Corinthians 4:8-10,16-18 NLT
2 Kings 9:30-32
2 Peter 1:3
Acts 2:17
Deuteronomy 11:14-15
Ecclesiastes 3:1
Ecclesiastes 3:1 NLT
Ephesians 4:25-28
Exodus 15:1
Exodus 20:2-3
Ezekiel 16:7
Galatians 5:22-23
Genesis 1:12 and 29
Genesis 1:14

Genesis 1:14-19
Genesis 2:9
Genesis 2:21
Genesis 3:18
Genesis 8:2
Genesis 8:21-22
Genesis 28:12
Isaiah 35:4
Isaiah 40:31
Isaiah 55:9
Isaiah 61:1-3
Isaiah 61:3
Matthew 10:39
Philippians 4:7
Proverbs 6:6-8
Proverbs 14:27
Proverbs 25:11-12 NLT
Psalm 56:13
Psalm 104:19

More from Andrea M. Polnaszek

For more information about having the author speak
to your organization or group, please contact:
apolnaszek@mac.com
or visit her website **andreapolnaszek.com**

Follow her on Facebook:
facebook.com/andrea.polnaszek

and Twitter **@apolnaszek**

Books by Andrea M. Polnaszek, LCSW

Touch Stone: The Joshua Project
The Elijah Project: My Protector, My Provider
Living the Elijah Project 40 Day Devotional
The Elijah Project 2, A New Season
Living the Elijah Project, A New Season 40 Day Devotional
My Wish for Christmas: The Luke Project
My Christmas Story

From the Editor

Using gender-neutral language has become standard practice in both journalistic and academic writing. In an effort to be gender-aware we chose to alternate genders, using masculine pronouns in some places and feminine ones in others.

About the Author

Andrea M. Polnaszek is a Licensed Clinical Social Worker who has spent years helping children and their families communicate with each other and grow in God's love. She has a Master's in Social Work and a Certificate in Theology from Southern Baptist Theological Seminary. It has been a joy for Andrea to share her talents with the word in her film writing and producing debut, *Catching Faith*, available on Amazon. In November 2016, *Wish for Christmas* was added to her writing credits. Her *Elijah Project* book series has been an international success.

Andrea is a proud mother of three. She and her husband, Perry, pastor Fellowship Church in Chippewa Falls, Wisconsin, USA. Andrea enjoys long walks with her family by the beautiful Lake Wissota.